The Forever Forest

Kids Save a Tropical Treasure

Kristin Joy Pratt-Serafini
with Rachel Crandell

Dawn Publications

Morpho Butterfly
(Morpho peleides limpida)

Yum, yum, rotting fruit! Unlike most butterflies, which sip nectar from flowers, Blue Morphos love to uncurl their long proboscises into sweet rotting fruit and slurp up the juices through their straw-like tongues. The bright blue that flashes in the sunlight is not really blue. The iridescent color is created in your eye because of the shape and angle of the scales of the butterfly, not from pigment in the scales. Morphos are optical engineers! Their big wings flop slowly and create a "flash defense" by exposing the bright blue from the top of the wings, alternating with drab brown on the underside. They seem to appear and disappear in flashes. They are almost invisible when they land and close their wings.

Heliconia
(Heliconia monteverdensis)

Heliconia's bright red brachts attract humming-birds to the small yellow blossoms. But it takes a lot of energy for plants to make the color red— botanists say that red is an "expensive" color. So rather than make the red blossom and lose it over and over, Heliconia makes a red bract—a permanent part of the plant.

Peter scampered down the shady trail after the biggest butterfly he had ever seen.

It flapped through a patch of sunlight, showing off its shiny blue wings.

"Look, Mom — a Blue Morpho! I've seen it in books—but it's way bigger than I imagined!" Peter was taking in all the sights, smells and sounds of his first trip to a tropical rainforest.

Peter was excited to spend some of his summer break in Costa Rica with his mom. They had come all the way from Sweden to visit the Children's Eternal Rainforest, or *El Bosque Eterno de los Niños*. Peter just called it "the BEN."

"I think we're almost there," said Anna, jogging to catch up with her son. Her friends, Dwight and Rachel, had invited them to stay at their cabin on the edge of the BEN. A pair of Blue-Crowned Motmots called to each other. *Hoop-hoop* said one. *Hoop-hoop* said the other.

From the opposite side of the path, Peter saw it snap an insect out of the air. "Hoop-hoop!" called Peter, imitating the birds. Rachel heard them coming. "I see you've met the Motmots!" she said.

Blue-crowned Motmot
(*Momotus momota*)

The Blue-crowned Motmot has two things most other birds don't have. It has two long tail feathers that swing slowly back and forth like a pendulum. And its strong beak has edges like a saw blade perfect for catching and holding beetles, cicadas, spiders, butterflies, small lizards and even snakes. Often they whack their prey on a branch until it is quite dead before swallowing it. Motmots dig a long burrow in the ground with a nest at the end.

Strangler Fig
(Ficus tuerckheimii)

Did you ever see a tree that grows from the top down instead of up, whose roots dangle in the air? A monkey, a bat or a bird poops out the seed from fig fruits it has eaten while perched in a different tree. When the fig seed sprouts on a branch in the treetop, it sends down roots. Over decades the fig's aerial roots reach the ground and fuse, looking somewhat like pretzels. The fig doesn't actually "strangle" the host tree, but encloses and shades it until it eventually dies. As the host tree rots, it feeds the Strangler Fig creating buttress roots and helping it grow bigger and bigger until it finally becomes a hollow cylinder perfect for climbing up inside.

Brown Tent-making Bat
(Uroderma magnirostrum)

Why would a bat make a tent? And how? Bats need a protected place to roost during the day, but many rainforests don't have caves. What rainforests do have is lots of big leaves. Tent bats nibble along the mid vein of a large leaf, punching little holes until it is weakened enough to bend and droop, creating a tent-like roof under which they hang. They move to different leaves frequently and roost in small groups that help them stay warm. Half of Monteverde's 121 mammal species are bats. Unlike insect-eating bats in North America, many Costa Rican bats eat fruit. They are a big help in replanting the forest because they poop as they fly. The seeds get dropped in open areas and regrow the forest.

The last of the sunlight filtered down through the blooming orchids clinging to the towering trees surrounding the cabin. "What's that thing growing around this tree?" Peter asked.

"A Strangler Fig, Peter," Rachel replied. "Eventually it will totally cover the big tree. When the tree rots away, the hollow place inside will make a perfect home for all kinds of rainforest animals." *Wow,* thought Peter. *The inside of a Strangler would be an awesome place for a hideout!*

It was getting dark fast. Dwight had dinner waiting. They ate on the porch and watched the Brown Tent-making Bats flap around, feasting on fruit. Peter was full of questions. "Why is it called the Children's Eternal Rainforest?" he asked. Rachel grinned. "Your mom knows the answer to that question."

"A long time ago," said his mom, "a second grade class learned about the animals and plants that live in the rainforest. They wanted to protect this place forever for the kids of the future."

Rachel served fried bananas in chocolate sauce for dessert. Just like Peter, Kinkajous also love bananas, even very ripe ones. A mother Kinkajou and her baby sat on the roof, eating bananas that they had picked from a nearby tree. They curled their tails around their feet and blinked their big eyes in the dusk. The baby Kinkajou was a very messy eater. He got banana slop all over his face! But don't worry—he had a super-long tongue, so he just licked the rest of his dinner off his nose!

Kinkajou
(Potos flavus)

When you think of pollinators, you probably picture bees and wasps. Did you know that mammals can be pollinators, too? The Kinkajou with its very long, pointy tongue can reach deep within large blossoms for nectar. At the same time it gets pollen all over its nose. Heading for the next blossom, and the next, the Kinkajou spreads the pollen through the forest canopy. It loves juicy fruits and sometimes hangs upside down by its prehensile tail to catch the drips. But their favorite food is wild figs. Another cool feature the Kinkajou has is hind feet that can turn backwards! That way its claws can grip when it climbs down a tree headfirst. These members of the raccoon family communicate by barks, chittering, and shrill quavering calls. They also scent mark from glands in bare places on the sides of their faces, at the corner of their mouths, on their throats and tummies. They rub these glands on branches to communicate with other Kinkajous.

Paca
(*Agouti paca*)

The best thing about Pacas is that they are so delicious. The worst thing about Pacas is that there aren't very many left. Hunters love to eat Paca and also get top dollar for Paca meat in the market. Outside of protected areas Pacas are hard to find. They are nocturnal, well-camouflaged, and quiet as they forage for fruits, roots, stems, seeds and leaves in the night. Their huge eyes help them see in the dark. Pacas are the largest rodents in Central America. When male Pacas defend their territories, they try to bluff the other Paca by rumbling and teeth chittering. If that doesn't work, they stand head-to-head slashing at each other with their large incisors. Pacas like to be near streams so they can escape into the water in time of danger. Pacas are good swimmers. They even poop in the water on purpose so predators can't track and find them by scent as easily. Pretty smart!

"So how could a class of kids protect this whole big forest?" Peter asked.

"They did things that kids can do!" his mom replied. "They put on a puppet show, sold tickets, and gave the money to buy some rainforest."

Dwight cleared away some dishes and spread out a map on the table. "See, Peter? Here's what happens when kids work together. Look how big the BEN is now!" Peter was amazed. And sleepy.

As Peter put on his pajamas, he spotted a Paca poking around the porch. He slid into his sleeping bag, and listened to the rain pattering on the roof.

Peter thought he might sleep in a little bit. After all, he was on vacation. The Mantled Howler Monkeys didn't have the same idea. It was barely light when a troop of about 10 monkeys moved through the trees, singing their morning wakeup song as loud as they could. "*Whooooaaa Hooh Hooh Hoooh!*"

Peter jumped out of bed and opened the curtains to see what was going on. A baby Howler was hanging by his tail from a tree branch. *These guys are really silly*, thought Peter. SPLAT! A sloppy piece of fruit hit the window and slid down the glass. Peter laughed. He decided not to throw his breakfast back at the Howler Monkeys. He knew Rachel and Dwight planned a big hike for today.

Mantled Howler Monkey
(Alouatta palliata)

What makes the Howler Monkey the loudest land animal on the planet? A specialized bone made of soft cartilage vibrates inside the Howler's large throat chamber. Just like a cello makes a deeper sound than a smaller violin with its larger hollow resonator, so the Howler's enlarged throat chamber helps create an enormous roar heard for miles across the rainforest. Every morning the alpha male in each troop of Howlers bellows out his "dawn chorus" to let other troops know where his group is feeding for the day. The Howler uses its prehensile tail to grip and hold. Monkeys in the Old World (Africa and Asia) don't have prehensile tails. Using their strong tails as a fifth arm, Howlers can dangle and reach more of their favorite leaves and fruits.

Hoffman's Two-toed Sloth
(Choloepus hoffmanni)

Who has two toes on the front and three toes on the back? You would know if you had ever "hung out" with a sloth. A Two-toed Sloth is a very slo-o-o-ow mammal with really long arms. An entire ecosystem lives in its fur, especially algae, making it look like a green blob of moss. Sloth moths also live in the fur. Once a week, the sloth climbs to the ground to defecate, and the moths fly out of its fur and lay their eggs on the poop. When they mature, the new sloth moths will fly away to find another sloth. Sloths have a difficult time walking, but their shoulders are formed perfectly for hanging upside down.

Orchids
(this one is Oerstedella centradenia)

Many trees in the BEN are covered with hundreds of varieties of orchids that are "air plants" or epiphytes—plants that never touch the ground. Some orchid blossoms are so tiny you'll need a magnifying glass to see them. Some flower for only a day or two. Many grow only in the top of the canopy and can't be seen from the ground. Scientists keep discovering new orchids as they explore the canopy.

Anna and Dwight loaded backpacks into the jeep. As they drove to the trailhead, Peter noticed that a fine mist hung in the air. It wasn't raining, but water dripped from the tip of every leaf. *So that's why they call this a cloud forest,* Peter thought. *I've always wondered what it's like to be inside a cloud!*

As soon as they started hiking, Peter became so busy looking with his binoculars, that he walked straight into Anna's backpack! Then he saw something odd. "There's a pile of moss up in that tree," he said. "Hey! The moss has arms!"

"That's not a moss, Peter, it's a sloth!" Anna said.
"And it's covered with algae, not moss." added Rachel.
Wow…that's the best camouflage I've ever seen, thought Peter.

Resplendent Quetzal
(Pharomachrus mocinno)

Ancient Maya people believed there was a creature that was half bird and half snake, a feathered serpent. Try saying its name… Quetzalcoatl! (Ket-sal-co-AH-tel) Its glittering feathers change color in the sunlight. Its tail feathers are so long and graceful that ancient Maya kings wore them as a royal headdress. The males show off by flying high into the air above the forest and nosediving straight down into the trees. Quetzals are great spitters. Their favorite food, the tiny wild avocados, have large seeds that quetzals spit out—which is a great help in replanting the forest.

The Elfin Forest

High winds sweep across the mountaintop, so only gnarly dwarf-sized trees can survive here—tall trees would blow over. Blasting winds drive clouds through the elfin forest, leaving it dripping wet, the perfect home for mosses, bromeliads, ferns and orchids. Costa Rica is the "orchid capital of the world" with over 1500 different species, many of them epiphytes.

Soon they stood on the top of a narrow ridge. Damp clouds rolled over the hills, watering the lush forests that stretched out below them in both directions. They were standing on the continental divide —water on one side flowed to the Atlantic Ocean, while water on the other side flowed to the Pacific. A Resplendent Quetzal swooped overhead. Peter got a good look at the bird's bright red breast and trailing green tail feathers.

It was hard to believe that one second grade class could protect this whole rainforest.

"Mom, are the kids that started the BEN still in school?" he asked. "I don't think so," she replied. "One of them became your mom!"

"Mom, your class was really awesome," said Peter, as they hiked down to the San Gerardo Field Station, where they would spend the night.

"We had a great class, Peter, but it wasn't just us," she replied. "We told our friends, and they told their friends, and before long there were kids from several countries all working together."

"Children from 44 countries all over the world have sent donations to the BEN," said Dwight. "Their help has made it grow much bigger."

"Wow, that's so—" *BONK! squeak.* "What's that?" The noise was so loud that Peter covered his ears. *BONK! squeak.* "That's a Three-wattled Bellbird," shouted Rachel over the racket. "One of the loudest birds on the planet!" *If only the Bellbird could travel around the world,* Peter thought, *it would really spread word about the BEN.*

Three-wattled Bellbird
(Procnias tricarunculata)

Most birds attract females with their beautiful songs or their colorful feathers, but the Three-wattled Bellbird has unique strategies. His common name could be "Loudmouth" as his distinctive call can be heard a mile away. He usually perches on a bare branch high above the treetops and calls to attract females. If a younger male tries to take over the perch by landing on the outer part of the branch, the Three-wattled Bellbird will scoot his competitor closer and closer to the end of the branch and then open his beak and BONK right in the young Bellbird's ear until he falls off. May the loudest bird win! The Bellbird's other weird feature is his three long wormlike wattles that hang from the base of his beak.

Wild Avocado
(Ocotea tonduzii)

Wild avocados the size of olives are the favorite food of Bellbirds, Quetzals, Guans and many other species. There are over 70 kinds of wild avocado trees in the Monteverde forest.

BONK!

Baird's Tapir
(Tapirus bairdii)

What prehistoric animal has three toes on its back feet and four on the front? The tapir. And it looked much the same thirty-five million years ago as it does today, a true "living fossil." It's the largest mammal in the Neotropics (tropics of the New World or western hemisphere) and weighs as much as 3 or 4 grown men. In spite of its bulk, the tapir eats only leaves, seeds and fruit with the help of its funny nose and upper lip. The nose looks and acts a bit like a short elephant's trunk. Its upper lip is long and prehensile so it can reach and grab food. Because tapir are endangered when their forest habitat is lost, the Monteverde Conservation League chose a mother tapir and her baby to be the symbol of the Children's Eternal Rainforest where tapir DO still live.

A little while later, the hikers stopped for a water break. They sat quietly for a few minutes to rest and listen to the sounds of the forest. *I wonder how I could help the rainforest?* Peter thought.

Suddenly, Dwight pointed into the trees. Nobody said a word. A big mama Baird's Tapir lumbered through the underbrush, whistling softly to the tapir baby trotting by her side. Peter almost missed seeing the baby because it was covered with light spots and stripes, just like baby deer, so it blended with the dappled light of the rainforest.

Leaf-cutter Ants
(Atta cephalotes)

*Did you know Leaf-cutter Ants are farmers?
They cut and carry the leaves to their huge underground colonies. They chew the leaves up and use
them as a fluffy "soil" in their garden. This special
fungus is the ants' only food and is found nowhere
else in the world. One queen ant has millions of
workers in her colony. Much like T-shirts, the
workers come in three sizes: small, medium and
large. The large ants are soldiers that guard the
colony and protect the trails. The medium-
sized ants cut and carry the leaves and work
underground. The little ones are tiny hitchhikers
who ride on the cut leaves to protect the medium
ones from wasps who lay their eggs on the heads
of the medium-sized ants. When the wasp egg
hatches, the larva will eat the head of the worker
ant. So the hitchhiker's job is to get rid of the wasp
egg and protect the ant. That's teamwork. They
are also garbage collectors removing dead ant
bodies to special underground trash chambers.*

Peter was thinking it was lots easier to hike
down the hill than up it, when he noticed
a line of Leaf-cutter Ants marching back
and forth across the trail. "Don't step on
the Leaf-cutter Ants, anyone!" Peter
announced. The hikers crouched down
to watch the ants haul leaf pieces back to
their nests. Right next to the ant trail, he
saw several huge paw prints in the mud.

"Hey, check this out!" called Peter.
"Who made these tracks?"

"Too big for an Ocelot," said Anna.
"Too big for a Margay," said Rachel.
"That's a Jaguar," said Dwight. "You almost never see them, but there are a few that live in this area."
"A Jaguar?! Wow!" Peter loved Jaguars because they were so fast and powerful.
"It takes a healthy rainforest to support a Jaguar," said Rachel. "They need a lot of room to hunt. Definitely a good sign!"

Jaguar
(Panthera onca)

It's rare to see a Jaguar because they are usually active at night. Researchers have to be detectives. Some clues are scratches on tree bark where Jaguars have scraped their claws to mark territory, or scat (poop), or paw prints along the trail, even scent markings where a Jaguar has sprayed. It isn't necessary for biologists to tag Jaguars to tell them apart, because each cat has its very own "fingerprint" or pattern of spots. These spots are a perfect camouflage on the sun-speckled forest floor. As the largest cats in the new world tropics, ancient people revered them for their strength and gave them the name yaguar which means "he who kills with one leap." With their huge teeth and claws they stand at the top of the food chain and eat anything they want including tapir, peccary, deer, turtles, sloth, otter, fish, birds, paca, caimen, and reptiles. Unlike lions, they cannot roar, but they do growl and mew. Unlike most cats, Jaguars love water and are good swimmers. They hunt over huge areas. That is why we need to protect large tracts of forest.

Rufus-eyed Stream Frog
(Duellmanohyla rufioculis)

The Rufous-eyed Stream Frog could be called the "Mystery Frog." No one knows exactly what it eats or where the female goes in the daytime. She's difficult to see because she is small, closes her big rusty-reddish eyes, and flattens her body against a leaf the same color she is. Perfect camouflage!

What we do know is they have sticky round pads on the tips of their toes to grip on slippery leaves. The male calls from his leafy perch just above the stream to attract females. His call sounds like two pebbles knocking together. Toxic chemicals in their skin protect them from predators.

Endemic to Costa Rica, they live in a few areas at the head of streams deep in the forest. "Endemic" means lives in only one place in the world. The Childrens' Eternal Rainforest is one of the most important protected refuges for them.

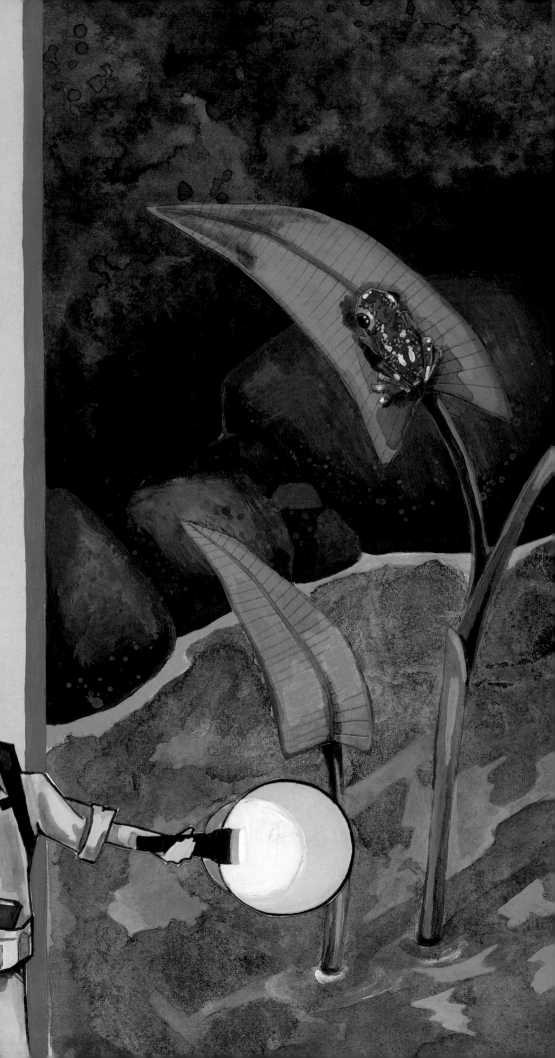

The hikers arrived at the San Gerardo Field Station just in time for dinner. Then Mark, a British naturalist, took them on a night hike. At first, Peter couldn't stop talking about all the animals and plants he had seen during the daytime. But he didn't want to miss all the night animals, so he started listening instead. After walking for a while, they stood still and turned off their flashlights. Peter tried to count the sounds. *Dripping water, insects, bats, frogs, my own breathing...*

Mark explained what they were hearing. "That's a Dink Frog...there's the Spot-Shouldered Rain Frog, and right here..." Mark flipped on his flashlight in the direction of the headwater of a tiny stream "...are two Rufous-eyed Stream Frogs. You're not likely to find them outside of Monteverde. The Rufous-Eyed Stream Frog might not have survived without the BEN."

Peter spent the rest of the night thinking about how to help the BEN.

He thought about the Blue Morphos and the Blue-crowned Motmots.
He thought about the Strangler Figs and the Brown Tent-making Bats.
He thought about the wide-eyed Kinkajous and the sneaky Pacas.
He thought about the noisy Howler Monkeys in the morning.
He thought about the Two-toed Sloths, and Three-wattled Bellbirds.
He thought about the baby Baird's Tapir and the Resplendent Quetzal.
He thought about the speedy Leaf-cutter Ants, the stealthy Jaguar…
　　　　　　　　and the teeny-tiny Rufous-eyed Stream Frog…

Reforestation

Although the BEN protects over 50,000 acres, it is only an "island" of rainforest. Beyond its borders, vast areas have been cut to raise crops and cattle, leaving a patchwork of isolated forests remaining. Many animals will not or cannot move through open fields—they need the forest for food and protection. The BEN and its associated organizations are working to connect these islands of forest by planting corridors that link the remaining forest. Tree roots also hold the soil in place and help streams to keep flowing. When native trees, like wild avocadoes, are replanted, migrating birds, like quetzals, can safely get to the food sources they need when the seasons change. Hundreds of thousands of baby trees have been given to farmers to plant as windbreaks and corridors. Hundreds of volunteers have helped replant, too.

...then he knew just how he could help!

This is the 1987 first and second grade class in Fagervik, Sweden, with their teacher Eha Kern, that had the idea to save a tropical rainforest by raising money to buy the land.

Rachel Crandell peers out from an opening in a hollow strangler fig tree.

Dwight and Rachel Crandell's cabin in Monteverde, Costa Rica.

How the Children's Eternal Rainforest Came to Be...

In 1951, a group of American Quakers who were looking for a peace-loving country to live in, immigrated to Costa Rica. They purchased 15,000 acres of mountainous rainforest and set aside 5,000 of those acres as Costa Rica's first rainforest preserve. They named it El Bosque Eterno, The Eternal Forest. They named their community Monteverde, or "Green Mountain."

In 1972, biologist George Powell went to Monteverde to study the resplendent quetzal. He deemed this cloud forest so special that he encouraged conservation organizations to protect more land in the area. Especially with the help of Wolf Guindon, one of the Quakers, the Monteverde Cloud Forest Preserve was created.

In 1987, the first and second grade students in Eha Kern's class in Fagervik, Sweden were learning about tropical rainforests. They were fascinated by the amazing array of wildlife, but were concerned when they learned that many of the rainforests were being cut and burned to make way for farms. An American botanist, Professor Sharon Kinsman of Bates College in Lewiston, Maine, was visiting Sweden. She knew the Monteverde Cloud Forest Preserve and was excited about the biodiversity she found there. Eha invited Sharon to tell the class about it.

When that class in Fagervik, Sweden learned about the rainforest, they wanted to do something to help. They decided to raise money. They put on a play and sold tickets. They organized a bunny-hopping contest. They gave pony rides. They sold home-baked goodies. Their goal was to raise enough money to buy and save 25 acres, but their enthusiasm grew and so did their fundraising ideas. A newspaper article was written about their efforts, then a television report was aired. Other kids heard about it, and more schools began to raise funds too. The Swedish government matched funds raised by the children. In the first year they raised over $100,000. That is how the Children's Rainforest (Barnens Regnskog in Swedish) was born.

Sharon helped arrange for threatened forest to be added to the BEN. She also founded "Children's Rainforest USA" to help kids in the United States participate in the campaign. The idea swept the world. Eventually, children in 44 countries contributed. Bernd Kern, Eha's husband, helped the international efforts by keeping people in touch and helping to set up sister organizations in Sweden, Germany, United Kingdom, Canada and Japan. By 1995, El Bosque Eterno de los Niños ("Children's Eternal Rainforest" in Spanish) commonly called the BEN, protected 54,000 acres and had become the largest private reserve in Central America.

Unfortunately, it was necessary to hire guards to protect the forest. Otherwise, poachers would illegally hunt animals for meat and for their pelts, or steal endangered orchids to sell to collectors, or catch colorful frogs and birds to sell as pets, or cut and sell endangered trees. Sometimes they even tried to clear land and plant crops inside the BEN!

In addition, rainforest corridors need to be created so that as the dry and wet seasons change, animals can migrate down from the mountaintops in the BEN to find food in the few remaining patches of undisturbed rainforest at lower altitudes. To help, the Monteverde Conservation League U.S. (MCLUS) was founded in 2002 to help raise money for additional land purchase, more guards, and environmental education. Also a group of enthusiastic students in Vermont began to raise money for critical habitat—they call themselves the "Change the World Kids." By 2007, the 20th anniversary of the BEN, the MCLUS had raised over a quarter of a million dollars. Children around the world are beginning to write the next chapter of this story.

Edmund Burke once said, "Nobody makes a greater mistake than he who does nothing because he could only do a little." Thanks go to the little Swedish kids long ago who chose to do something. They began to protect tropical rainforest and many friends have helped since. Now the Children's Eternal Forest has a chance to be a forest ... forever.

May the forest be with you,

Rachel & Kristin

Special thanks to the friends and biologists who helped us make this book as accurate as possible:
Judy Arroyo, Federico Chinchilla, Dwight Crandell,
Deb DeRosier, Frank Joyce, Eha Kern, Sharon Kinsman,
Richard Laval, Carlos Muñoz, Giselle Rodriguez,
Mark Wainwright, Jim Wolfe, Willow Zuchowski.

KRISTIN PAINTING THE TITLE PAGE FOR 'THE FOREVER FOREST' - RIGHT IN THE BEN!

HUNDREDS OF BABY TREES READY TO BE PLANTED IN PLACES WHERE THE RAINFOREST WAS CHOPPED DOWN

SAN GERARDO FIELD STATION

How To Learn More About Tropical Rainforests:

Books:

Children Saved the Rain Forest by Dorothy Patent (1996):

    Packed with information about the cloud forest, this book celebrates the Swedish children who started the BEN.

A Walk in the Rainforest by Kristin Joy Pratt (1992):

    This is an alphabet book written on two levels—for young children as well as for older children or adults, which follows XYZ the Ant on his walk through the forest.

The Great Kapok Tree by Lynne Cherry (1990):

    This lushly illustrated book introduces the reader to the animal families of a Brazilian rainforest, with a plea for protection.

Flute's Journey by Lynne Cherry (1997):

    A neo-tropical migrating wood thrush makes a perilous journey from the Children's Eternal Rainforest in Costa Rica to Maryland.

When the Monkeys Came Back by Kristine Franklin (1994):

    This book traces the life of Doña Marta and how she replants the forest and restores the wildlife.

The Lorax by Dr. Seuss (1971, 2004):

    Here is the classic story of foolish waste of a forest and loss of biodiversity with a ray of hope at the end.

The Cloud Forest by Sneed Collard (2001):

    This is a beautifully illustrated close-up look at the plants and animals that inhabit the Monteverde cloud forest.

It's Our World Too by Phillip Hoose (1993):

    This collection of true stories about children who have helped the world be a better place includes a story about the BEN which begins on page 83 .

Websites:

Monteverde Conservation League US, Inc.
    www.mclus.org

Monteverde Conservation League
    www.acmcr.org

Monteverde Cloud Forest Preserve
    www.cloudforestalive.org

Costa Rican Conservation Foundation
    www.fccmonteverde.org

Change the World Kids
    www.changetheworldkids.com

Children's Rainforest of Sweden
    www.barnens-regnskog.net

Children's Rainforest U.K.
    www.tropical-forests.com

Children's Rainforest Japan
    www.jungle.rg.jp

Children's Rainforest Germany
    www.kinderregenwald.de

Roots and Shoots, Jane Goodall's program for youth
    www.rootsandshoots.org

Rainforest Action Network,
    www.ran.org/what_we_do/rainforessts_in_the_classroom

Rainforest Alliance
    www.rainforest-alliance.org/programs/education/

Missouri Botanical Garden
    www.mbgnet.net

To Find the BEN on Google Earth, fly to 10 22' N, 84 43' W and click on search. Look for the big dark green patch of forested mountains south of Arenal Volcano and the big lake. Click on the nearby blue dots for photos of scenes near the BEN.

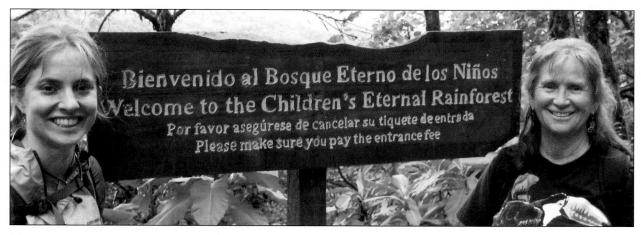

MARCH 2007: KRISTIN JOY PRATT-SERAFINI AND RACHEL CRANDELL HIKE THROUGH THE BEN DOWN TO THE SAN GERARDO FIELD STATION, JUST LIKE PETER DOES IN THE STORY.

Kristin Joy Pratt-Serafini

www.xyzant.com

Kristin Joy Pratt-Serafini first connected her love of art with her concern for the rainforest when she wrote and illustrated A Walk in the Rainforest as a freshman in high school. Since then, she has written and illustrated several other environmentally-focused books for children. She hopes her colorful paintings will get kids excited about going outside and exploring for themselves. Kristin first visited the BEN in 1997 as a college student, and was excited to go back with Rachel 10 years later, in March of 2007. As she wrote the story about Anna and Peter, and painted the animals and plants they saw, she could picture every step of their adventure through the rainforest... because she had just been to the BEN herself! Rachel took her on the same hike described in the story. She even saw the Rufous-eyed Stream Frogs on the night hike with Mark!

Rachel Crandell

www.rainforestrachel.com

Rachel Crandell taught at Principia Lower School for 20 years after running a nursery school on their farm in Indiana. She and her husband started the Monteverde Conservation League, U.S. to help protect the Children's Eternal Rainforest. They have a cabin in Monteverde where they spend several months each year. Just like Peter and Anna in the story, her children and grand-children have walked the paths, climbed the strangler fig, and heard the bellbird BONK. Besides researching and writing the scientific paragraphs for The Forever Forest, Rachel has motivated thousands of children and adults to help protect the BEN. She is known as "Rainforest Rachel" because of the hundreds of presentations she has done for school groups about tropical rainforests, and the trips she leads to Costa Rica.

Copyright © 2008
Kristin Joy Pratt-Serafini and Rachel Crandell
Illustrations copyright © 2008 Kristin Joy Pratt-Serafini

A Sharing Nature With Children Book

Computer production by Patty Arnold, *Menagerie Design and Publishing*.

Dawn Publications
12402 Bitney Springs Road, Nevada City, CA 95959
530-274-7775 • nature@dawnpub.com

Printed in China
10 9 8 7 6 5 4 3 2 1
First Edition

Library of Congress Cataloging-in-Publication Data
Pratt-Serafini, Kristin Joy.
  The forever forest : kids save a tropical treasure / Kristin Joy Pratt-Serafini, with Rachel Crandell ; illustrated by Kristin Joy Pratt-Serafini.
    p. cm.
  Summary: "On a hike through the Children's Eternal Rain-forest, Peter discovers many intriguing plants and animals, and also that his mother was one of the second-graders who joined with other children from all over the world to make preserva-tion of this Costa Rican rainforest possible"--Provided by publisher.
  Includes bibliographical references and index.
  ISBN-13: 978-1-58469-101-3 (hardback : alk. paper)
  ISBN-13: 978-1-58469-102-0 (pbk. : alk. paper)
  1. Bosque Eterno de los Niños (Costa Rica)--Juvenile literature. 2. Rain forest ecology--Costa Rica--Bosque Eterno de los Niños. I. Crandell, Rachel. II. Title.
  QH108.C6P73 2008
  578.734097286--dc22
                                          2007035606

ALSO BY KRISTIN JOY PRATT-SERAFINI

A Walk in the Rainforest—colorful, fresh and now a classic, this was illustrated with magic markers when Kristin was 15 years old.

A Swim through the Sea—using the same alliterative, alphabetical approach as her rainforest book, this was illustrated with watercolors when Kristin was 17 years old.

A Fly in the Sky—similar in style to the previous two books, this title explores birds, insects and other curious animals that fly, illustrated when Kristin was 19 years old.

Salamander Rain: A Lake and Pond Journal—from a kid's eye view, this introduces the creatures of the wetlands through Kristin's model journal and scrapbook.

Saguaro Moon: A Desert Journal—similar in style to the wetlands book, this is a journal about the desert from a young woman who has become a naturalist in her own right.

SOME OTHER NATURE AWARENESS BOOKS FROM DAWN PUBLICATIONS

How We Know What We Know about Our Changing Climate by Lynne Cherry and Gary Braasch—clearly presents evidence of climate change including patterns from birds, flowers, tree rings, mud cores, and much more, and how evidence is often gathered by young "citizen-scientists."

Over in the Jungle: A Rainforest Rhyme, by Marianne Berkes, illustrated by Jeanette Canyon—this counting book captures a rain forest teeming with remarkable creatures.

Over in the Ocean: In a Coral Reef, illustrated by Jeanette Canyon —with unique and outstanding style, this book portrays the vivid community of creatures that inhabit the ocean's coral reefs.

Eliza and the Dragonfly by Susie Caldwell Rinehart, illustrated by Anisa Claire Hovemann—a charming story of a girl and a dragonfly, each experiencing their own metamorphosis.

If You Give a T-Rex a Bone, by Tim Myers, illustrated by Anisa Claire Hovemann—takes you back to ancient habitats that are, well—interesting. Dangerously interesting!

The Web at Dragonfly Pond, by Brian "Fox" Ellis, illustrated by Michael S. Maydak—a real-life story of fishing with father that reveals how nature's food chain is connected.

Dawn Publications is dedicated to inspiring in children a deeper understanding and appreciation for all life on Earth. To view our titles or to order, please visit us at www.dawnpub.com, or call 800-545-7475.

SAMUEL SLATER'S MILL

AND THE INDUSTRIAL REVOLUTION

Turning Points
IN AMERICAN HISTORY

SAMUEL SLATER'S MILL

AND THE INDUSTRIAL REVOLUTION

Christopher Simonds

Silver Burdett Press, Inc.
Englewood Cliffs, New Jersey

Acknowledgments

The editor thanks the following individuals and institutions for their invaluable help in text and picture research: Mr. Wade Lawrence, the Historical Society of York County, Pennsylvania; Mr. Robert Macieski, the Slater Mill Historical Site; and Mr. Louis L. Tucker, Massachusetts Historical Society.

Consultant

Richard M. Haynes
Assistant Professor
Division of Administration, Curriculum and Instruction
Director of the Office of Field Experiences and Teacher
  Placement, School of Education and Psychology
Western Carolina University

Cover: An early view of Samuel Slater's first mill at Pawtucket, Rhode Island. Smithsonian Institution.

Title Page: A steam train travels through the peaceful countryside in this 1855 painting, The Lackawanna Valley. *George Innes; National Gallery of Art, Washington; gift of Mrs. Huttleston Rogers.*

Contents Page: Women and children weave cloth on an early power loom. Smithsonian Institution.

Back Cover: An early trademark of one of the Lowell, Massachusetts Textile Mills. Courtesy of the Museum of American Textile History.

Library of Congress Cataloging-in-Publication Data

Simonds, Christopher.
   Samuel Slater's mill and the Industrial Revolution/Christopher Simonds.
      p.   cm. —(Turning points in American History.)
      Includes bibliographical references (p.   ).
      Summary: A biography of the Englishman who left for America despite laws forbidding the emigration of textile workers and established the American textile industry.
      1. Slater, Samuel, 1768-1835—Juvenile literature.
   2. Industrialists—United States—Biography—Juvenile literature.
   3. Textile industry—United States—History—Juvenile literature.
   [1. Slater, Samuel, 1768-1835. 2. Industrialists. 3. Textile industry—United States—History.] I. Title. II. Series: Turning points in American history. (Englewood Cliffs, N.J.)
   HD9860.S5S56   1990
   338.7'67221'092—dc20
   [B]   90-30907
   [92]   CIP
                                                            AC

Editorial Coordination by Richard G. Gallin

Created by Media Projects Incorporated

C. Carter Smith, *Executive Editor*
Toni Rachiele, *Managing Editor*
Charles A. Wills, *Project Editor*
Bernard Schleifer, *Design Consultant*
Arlene Goldberg, *Cartographer*

ISBN 0-382-09951-6 [lib. bdg.]
10 9 8 7 6 5 4 3 2 1

ISBN 0-382-09947-8 [pbk.]
10 9 8 7 6 5 4 3 2 1

CONTENTS

INTRODUCTION

A SPY COMES TO NEW YORK

The tall young man walked away from the sailing ship that had brought him from England to the New World. Solid ground must have felt strange underfoot after sixty-six days at sea. Strange, too, were the sights, sounds, and smells of New York, for young Samuel Slater had lived all his life in the English countryside. He looked like nothing more than another English farmer come to try his luck in a new land.

Slater might never have made it out of England if the authorities had known what he really was: a factory manager, a mechanical genius, and—most important—a spy. In his head he carried a complex pattern of shafts, wheels, gears, and spindles—a pattern that would change people's lives in ways that no one could then imagine.

New York as it looked when Samuel Slater arrived. The building on the left is the Tontine coffeehouse, an early business center.

Slater brought with him to America the secret of making cotton thread quickly and cheaply by machine. For centuries, cotton and other textiles had been made with hand tools in the home. Women first carded the raw cotton fibers with metal combs. Then the cotton was spun by hand on a spinning wheel. Spinning produced a strong thread that was woven on a loom into cloth.

In the 1760s, the Englishman Richard Arkwright invented the water-powered spinning frame. This new machine brought cotton spinning out of the home and into the factory. Water wheels turned by rushing streams replaced human muscle power, and each frame, tended by one worker, replaced several spinning wheels.

Factories cost money. In 1771, Arkwright persuaded Jedediah Strutt, a wealthy farmer, to provide the cash he needed to build machines and mills. By 1776 (the year thirteen of England's

Before the invention of water- and steam-powered mills, fiber was spun into thread at home.

American colonies revolted), Arkwright's and Strutt's mills had more than 5,000 workers. Young Samuel Slater lived within walking distance of two of these mills. His father was an old friend of Strutt's, so no one minded when the boy hung around. Samuel was fascinated by the whirling, rattling, clanking machinery. In 1782, Strutt built a new mill just a mile from the Slater farm. Samuel, then aged fourteen, landed a job there as a clerk. A year later, he signed on as an apprentice, agreeing to live with Strutt and work in the mill until he was twenty-one.

Richard Arkwright's water-powered spinning frame helped begin the Industrial Revolution in Britain. This is a replica of a 1775 model.

The English village of Belper, where Samuel Slater was born in 1768. The big building on the right is Strutt's mill, where Slater worked before coming to America.

By the time he reached that age, he knew all there was to know about cotton-spinning machinery. He felt ready to strike out on his own, but he lacked the money to build his own mill with the latest machinery. Then he learned that in America, a bounty of 100 English pounds (about $500) had recently been paid to the designer of a cloth-making machine. Slater saw that the newly independent United States offered him a golden opportunity.

There was one problem: the law. England wanted to keep the new art of cloth manufacturing, and the huge profits from it, to itself. Since 1774, it had been illegal to send textile machinery, or the plans for it, out of England. The penalty was a fine of 200 English pounds or twelve years in jail.

But Samuel Slater needed no machinery or plans. The information was all in his head. Because an experienced mill superintendent might be kept from leaving England, he played the part of a farmer. He left home on September 1, 1789, and arrived in New York late in November.

1

NEW WORLD, OLD WAYS

The town Samuel Slater came to in 1789 was much different from the New York City of today. Pigs ran in the unpaved streets, the tallest buildings were only three or four stories, and the usual way of getting rid of garbage was to throw it out the nearest window. Comforts that we take for granted—like streetlights, sewers, clean drinking water—were unheard of. The population was 28,000.

Yet this cramped, noisy, smelly town was briefly the capital of the United States. A few months before, George Washington had been sworn in there as the first president. Only Philadelphia had more people, and only three other cities had populations over 8,000: Boston, Baltimore, and Charleston. In the whole nation, there were only twenty-four cities of more than 2,500 people.

George Washington was inaugurated as the first president of the United States a few months before Samuel Slater arrived.

Out of a population of just under 4 million, only 200,000 lived in cities or towns; the rest were farmers in the countryside. The five "big cities" were all seaports; most other towns had grown up near the sea, or near rivers that could be used to transport people and goods.

Whether townspeople or farmers, most of the 4 million Americans lived on a strip of land that ran along the Atlantic coast from southern Maine to northern Georgia. This settled land extended westward only as far as the foothills of the Appalachian Mountains. In and beyond the mountains lay a forest that stretched unbroken to the banks of the Mississippi River. Only Native Americans, fur traders, and a few families of pioneers lived in this wilderness.

Even on that strip between seacoast and mountains, the people of the new nation were thinly spread. They had little contact with one another. The only means of communication was the mail,

COURTESY, AMERICAN ANTIQUARIAN SOCIETY

This poster advertises a Boston–New York stage-coach line. In 1815, the trip took more than a day and a half.

which was slow and unreliable. Newspapers took days, often weeks, to reach their scattered readers. Land transportation was difficult: The 200-mile trip from New York City to Boston, which we make in four hours by train or car today, took a fast stagecoach six days— *if* the roads were clear and the weather was good. It was easier, safer, and more comfortable to go from place to place by boat, along the seacoast or up and down the rivers.

It was also expensive to move people and, especially, goods. Because of the lack of roads, it cost more to transport a ton of freight from western New York State to New York City than it cost to ship the same ton from New York City 3,000 miles across the sea to London.

Americans in 1789 lived pretty much the way their parents and grandparents had lived before them. Dwellers in the coastal cities and towns depended on oceangoing trade. They built and equipped the sailing ships that carried goods between the New World and the Old. Merchants shipped food and raw materials—furs, tobacco, iron, tar, lumber—to Europe and the West Indies. Their ships returned with finished products—hardware, woolen cloth, fine furniture, wine, silk—which they sold at a profit.

Some farmers in the southern states and the Hudson River valley of New York built large plantations. Slaves or (in the North) tenant farmers on these plantations produced a surplus of food and livestock, which was sold in the cities to be used there or to be shipped overseas.

The typical American farm family, however, did not try to produce a surplus or make a profit. Instead, it was self-sufficient: The farm provided just about everything a family needed to survive. A farmer cut down trees and shaped them into lumber, which he (and his neighbors, if there were any) built into house and barns. The family

A farm wife slaughters a pig in this eighteenth-century drawing.

raised corn or wheat to feed themselves and their livestock. The only fresh fruits and vegetables they ate were those they could raise or find growing wild.

Farm animals provided milk, meat, eggs, wool, leather, candles, and muscle power for plowing and hauling. Farm wives spun wool on a spinning wheel, wove it, and sewed it to make clothing; clothes were washed in soap made on the farm from ashes and animal fat. More often than not, the farmer and his wife had to be doctor, schoolteacher, and preacher for their family, too.

If the farmer's life was hard, his wife's was harder. Besides cooking, baking, washing, spinning, sewing, and making cheese, butter, soap, and a dozen other necessities, she cared for and educated the many children needed to work the farm.

There were some goods and services that the farm family could not provide for itself. Every few weeks, the farmer had to travel to the nearest settlement—usually a few buildings at a crossroads—to buy manufactured goods like nails, kitchenware, window glass, pins and needles, and buttons, as well as

Blacksmiths, who forged tools and other items from iron, were among the small, independent artisans of America in the eighteenth and nineteenth centuries.

salt, tea, and spices. Recently, the storekeeper had begun selling good-quality cotton cloth from England—at a low price, thanks to the new manufacturing process developed by Arkwright.

There, too, the farmer saw the only machinery most Americans of that time had any contact with: the mill, where a water wheel powered the grindstones that turned corn or wheat into meal or flour. If the miller was an up-to-date businessman, he had remodeled his mill on the design of a mechanically minded young American named Oliver Evans. Using Evans's system, two men could operate the mill, whereas four or five had been needed before.

Other Americans were artisans— skilled craftsworkers—who made the things farmers and merchants couldn't make for themselves. These people, who lived in towns and villages, included blacksmiths, carpenters, silversmiths, and gunsmiths. Artisans owned their own shops and relied on their families, as well as apprentices (young people who worked for free in order to learn a craft), for help. They took pride in their work and their independence. Along with farmers, artisans were examples of the independent, "republican" society that was the United States just after the Revolutionary War.

Though farm life was hard and often lonely, the typical American farmer of 1789 was no ignorant bumpkin. Even

Thomas Jefferson hoped the United States would stay a land of independent farmers and artisans.

Alexander Hamilton encouraged the growth of industry in the young United States.

though members of a farm family might never travel far from home, they could read. Newspapers and almanacs, though slow to reach the farm, made members of the farmer's family aware of the world beyond the family's fields. They understood the causes and events of the Revolution that had made them free American citizens instead of subjects of the English king. The farmer had followed the debate over the new Constitution that Congress had just adopted, and had probably voted in the election that made George Washington the first president.

The farmer and the artisan knew the views of Thomas Jefferson and his followers, who believed that for liberty to survive, the new nation should be a land of independent, hard-working landowners and artisans. The farmer and the artisan knew (and probably disagreed with) the opposing opinion of

Alexander Hamilton, the secretary of the treasury. Hamilton felt that although the United States had won its political independence in the Revolution, it remained a stepchild of the Old World. Europe, especially England, still used it as a source of raw materials and as a market for finished products. To end this second-class status, Hamilton wanted the federal government to give financial and other aid to American trade and industry.

Though the debate between Jeffersonians and Hamiltonians would rage for many years after 1789, the result was decided on the day Samuel Slater landed in New York. Slater and his head full of machinery would change the lives of our farm family and all of their fellow citizens. Farmers might remain on the land to the end of their days, but the farmers' children and grandchildren would grow up in an industrial nation.

2

"THEE SAID THEE COULD MAKE MACHINERY"

Samuel Slater had no trouble finding work in his adopted country. The New York Manufacturing Company was glad to hire a young man with his experience. This first job, however, was a disappointment. Slater had hoped to build cotton-spinning machinery, but the company was spinning flax to make linen, not cotton. Worse, the machinery was old and inefficient. This was no basis for developing a huge, busy mill like the ones he had worked in back in England.

After a few weeks, Slater heard about a rich merchant in Rhode Island, Moses Brown, who was trying to start a cotton-spinning mill. Slater fired off a letter:

A few days ago I was informed that you wanted a manager of *cotton-spinning*, etc., in which business I flat-

ter myself that I can give the greatest satisfaction, in making machinery, making good yarn . . . as I have had opportunity, and an oversight of Sir Richard Arkwright's works, and in Mr. Strutt's mill upward of eight years.

Moses Brown wrote back with a good offer. Slater would get a portion of the profits from the mill that Brown and his partners had put up the money to build and equip. However, the interest on that money would be deducted—that is, taken away from Slater's share of the profits.

Slater took the next boat to Providence, Rhode Island, where he met his future partner for the first time. The two went by horse-drawn sleigh to Pawtucket, a little village north of the city. There, in a rented building, Brown showed Slater the machinery he had bought for the new business. All Brown thought he needed was a mechanic to get the machinery in good running order.

Pawtucket, Rhode Island, as it appeared early in the nineteenth century.

Moses Brown

For Slater, this was another blow. He saw that Brown had bought badly made copies of English machinery that was already out of date. No wonder Brown hadn't yet made or sold an inch of cotton. The only bright spot was the river Slater could hear rushing by outside. The Blackstone River, he knew, would be a steady, dependable source of power for the mill of his dreams.

Slater told Brown the machinery wouldn't do. Legend has it that the old merchant replied, in the Quaker way of speaking, "Thee said thee could make machinery. Why not do it?"

But Slater had another problem. He wanted—and Brown had offered him—a partnership in the company. Instead of a weekly salary, he would receive half

of the profits. (Profit is the money a business has left over after goods are sold and expenses paid. A salary is a fixed amount of money that a worker earns for working a certain amount of time.) Thus, if the mill was successful and sold a lot of cotton, Slater would make more money than if he just received a salary. But how big would those profits be? Not very, if the company had to pay off the debt for the poor machinery Brown had bought. Slater was too smart a businessman to join a company that was burdened with debt.

The two men compromised. Slater would do what he could to improve the machinery; then they would work out a new partnership agreement.

Like most raw materials, cotton looks very different from the finished product. It comes from the field in fist-sized puffs of dirty-looking white fluff, and it takes several steps to make cotton into cloth.

First, the seeds have to be picked out. In 1790, slaves did this by hand on the cotton plantations.

Next, the cotton is *carded*—drawn between two wire brushes to get all the fibers running in the same direction.

Third, the mat of carded cotton goes through a *drawing* machine, which stretches and tightens it into a loose yarn called *sliver*.

Fourth, the sliver is wound onto large spools called *bobbins*. The bobbins are put on the *spinning frame*. Whirling *spindles* stretch the yarn more and also twist the strands of fiber. The twisting process makes the yarn strong enough to be woven into cloth on a *loom* or knitted on other machines.

Brown's plan was for the company to take orders for all kinds of cotton cloth. The mill Slater was hired to organize would do the carding, drawing, and spinning by water-powered machinery. The yarn it made would be turned over to weavers. Working at home on hand looms, they would turn the yarn into finished cloth, which the company would deliver to its customers.

Slater had a better idea, but first he had to get the machinery working. To do this, he needed a mechanic and a machine shop. He also needed a place to live.

Brown was able to take care of both needs. He took Slater to Oziel Wilkinson's home nearby. Wilkinson was a mechanic who had the skills and tools needed to make machinery. Slater would live in Wilkinson's house, and Wilkinson and his son David would help him adapt and improve Brown's machinery. It was there that Slater met Wilkinson's daughter Hannah, whom he married in 1792.

Hannah Wilkinson Slater was a remarkable person in her own right. She must have observed her father's work closely, for she had a great deal of mechanical ability. A year after marrying Samuel Slater, Hannah developed a new method for making cotton sewing thread. In 1793, Hannah Slater patented her improved thread-making process and became the first woman to be granted a patent by the U.S. government. Hannah Slater's invention would play an important role in the growth of America's textile industry, just as her husband's mill did.

Slater and the Wilkinsons set to work. By April 1790, thanks to Slater's excellent memory and his co-workers' skill, they had a spinning frame up and running that met Slater's high standards. Now he was ready to commit himself to a partnership. A new company, the firm of Almy, Brown & Slater, was set up. William Almy was Moses Brown's son-in-law; the third partner was Smith Brown, his cousin. Slater got half ownership of the new machinery and half of the mill's profits. The debt for the equipment Brown had bought was written off—that is, it would not be subtracted from Slater's share of the profits. Slater agreed to build two more spinning frames, a drawing frame, and two carding machines.

Such family partnerships were common in the early days of American manufacturing. Just as the farm family survived by working together, early industries were able to succeed because of the support family members gave one another. Families could combine their money to build factories—or, just as important, the labor to make the factories produce.

As it turned out, the simplest of the three machines, the carding machine, gave Slater and the Wilkinsons the most trouble. After eight months of hard work and trial and error, they at last got it right. All that was left to do was to lay in a supply of raw cotton and hook up the machinery.

HISTORY

OF THE

OLD CARD AND WATER FRAME

Presented to the "Rhode Island Society for the Encouragement of Domestic Industry."

Samuel Slater arrived in New York in January 1790. On the 18th of the same month he went to Pawtucket and commenced building the first machinery for the "Old Spinning Mill" and started the same in a clothier's shop by the power of the Fulling Mill wheel, December 20th 1790. viz: 3 Carding Machines.
Drawing and Roving machines.
1 Water Frame   24 Spindles.
1   do   do   48 Spindles.

Where they run for about twenty Months, and over-stocked the "Domestic Goods" market — Several thousand pounds of yarn having accumulated in that time notwithstanding the most active exertions on the part of the proprietors to dispose of the product both in yarns and in cloth woven by hand

The Spinning frame of 24 spindles was the first or experimental machine, and consequently imperfect, and taken from the Mill to give place to machines of more perfect Construction.

In 1793 William Almy, Obadiah M. Brown and Samuel Slater — under the firm of Almy, Brown & Slater — built a small Factory — the centre portion of the "Old Spinning Mill" into which the above mentioned machinery was removed and put in operation on the 12th of July of the same year

One of the carding machines and the 48 Spindle Water-frame mentioned above were presented as above by the heirs of Moses Brown, William Almy and Obadiah M. Brown, and now stand in State in the rooms of the society

Moses Brown was the foster-father of the whole enterprise — Almy, Brown & Slater were the owners and the recipients of the benefit arising therefrom.

Providence 9th Month 15th 1856.

Note The above facts are chiefly derived
from a Memo by Samuel Slater to
the R.I. Hist: Society. W.J.H.

Samuel Boyd Tobey —
Trustee and Attorney of Heirs aforesaid

This document from the Rhode Island Historical Society describes the early history of Slater's mills.

Power to run the carding, drawing, and spinning machines came from the river. Some of the water was drawn into a channel, called a *mill race*, that ran under the building. There it turned a large wooden wheel that looked like the paddlewheel of a steamboat. Gears transferred the motion of the turning wheel to a vertical shaft that ran up to the mill floor. There, that shaft turned other shafts, which moved leather belts attached to pulleys on the machines. In this way, one wheel turning in the water could run several separate machines. Each machine had several *spindles*. Each spindle drew and twisted cotton into yarn. In a mill like Slater's, the worker's job was to make sure that each spindle on his machine was continuously fed with cotton, and to remove the finished yarn as each spindle filled up. Sometimes the yarn broke, and the worker had to splice the two ends together.

One day in December 1790, Slater went down to the basement of the mill and broke up the ice that had frozen around the water wheel. The wheel turned slowly, the shaft began to spin, and upstairs the machinery began moving—and worked. On December 20, Slater's mill made the first cotton yarn ever produced by water-powered machinery in America. The mill had only 72 spindles on its spinning frames, in contrast to the thousands of spindles in an English mill, but it was a beginning.

To work in the mill, Slater hired seven boys and two girls, ages seven to twelve. One was Smith Wilkinson, soon to become his brother-in-law. Slater

A replica of a carding machine—one of the machines Slater built for Moses Brown.

knew from his experience in England that children, with their small, quick fingers, were the ideal workers to tend the fast-moving spinning machinery. Also, children worked for lower wages than adults. Besides, it was customary in those days for children to work, whether on the family farm, in the family business, or as apprentices to craftsmen. Still, not all parents were enthusiastic about sending their children to work in Slater's mill. In 1795, Slater wrote that it took "considerable and warm debate" to persuade a local man to let his children work.

Slater sent a sample of American yarn to his old employer, Samuel Strutt, in England. Strutt wrote back, praising the quality of Slater's product. At Moses Brown's suggestion, another sample

The first Slater mill as it looked in 1793. The Blackstone River is visible in the background.

went to Secretary of the Treasury Alexander Hamilton to show what the "infant industries" of the United States were capable of producing.

One of the first effects of Slater's mill was a reduction in the price of cotton in America. Cotton cloth woven from imported English yarn cost an American household 40 to 50 cents a yard. Almy, Brown & Slater could sell cloth that was just as good for as little as 9 cents a yard. The workers in Slater's mill made about 25 cents a day—not quite enough to buy a single piece of clothing made with that cloth.

The new product caught on quickly. In its first ten months of operation, the company sold almost 8,000 yards of cloth. In another ten months, the mill was turning out more yarn than all the weavers in the area could handle. As a surplus of yarn began to build up, the Browns begged Slater to slow down.

Now Slater faced a problem almost as tough as making the carding machine work. He had to teach his partners a whole new way of doing business.

Almy, Brown & Slater was producing cotton on what was called a *bespoke* basis. When a customer ordered so many yards of cloth, the company would spin the yarn needed and farm out the weaving. Slater knew that for the mill to make the largest possible profit (half of which was to be his), it had to run at full capacity and produce as much yarn as it possibly could. The company, he insisted, should sell yarn anywhere and everywhere, not just in its little corner of New England. It should forget about

A scene in one of Samuel Slater's early mills.

putting yarn out to weavers and selling finished cloth. Instead, it should concentrate on selling all the yarn it could make.

Now another side of Slater's English know-how appeared. Once the machinery was running properly, it was easily kept working. Any mechanic with an oil can and a little experience could do that. But to keep it running at full capacity took a *manager*. Slater was, above all, an outstanding manager of machinery and production. He knew how to control the flow of cotton through the mill. At no time was any machine idle because no one had brought it more cotton; never was one machine allowed to produce more than the next machine in the process could handle.

That kind of efficiency, Slater knew, would lead to maximum profits for himself and his partners. He used his skill as a manager to make the mill successful. The men who worked under him learned from his example, and many of them went on to set up mills of their own using his system.

Soon Slater's partners were convinced. The company began selling its yarn to agents in New York, Philadelphia, and Baltimore. The mill clanked away all day, every day, and by the end of 1792 Slater's share of the profits had totaled $5,000—a large sum in a time when the average skilled worker made $300 to $400 a year, and larger still than the wages earned by workers in Slater's mill.

In 1793, Almy, Brown & Slater opened a new, larger mill near their original building. By 1800, the mill employed a hundred workers. It expanded over the years until, in 1812, it had over 5,000 spindles producing cotton yarn. Soon, mills dotted the landscape of New England, and thousands of men, women, and children—often entire families—would leave small, unproductive farms to work in them. For decades, people had been tied to the land. In the seventeenth and eighteenth centuries, members of a farm family might never travel more than a few miles from their home. The mills began to change this. They brought *mobility*—movement—to New England society. A working family might move all the way to another state to find work. Or they might leave one mill for another if wages were higher. And as the mills prospered, towns sprang up along the rivers that provided power. Slater's innovations weren't just making cloth less expensive. They were changing the landscape and society of New England. In the next century, they would help do the same for the rest of the United States.

In 1794, Almy and the Browns set up another mill in Pawtucket. In 1797, Slater went into partnership with his in-laws, the Wilkinsons. This new firm, Samuel Slater & Co., built a mill across the river. In 1806, Slater's brother John, who had followed him to America, es-

The village of Slatersville, founded by John Slater in 1806. The inset shows the swift-moving water that made New England ideal for mills.

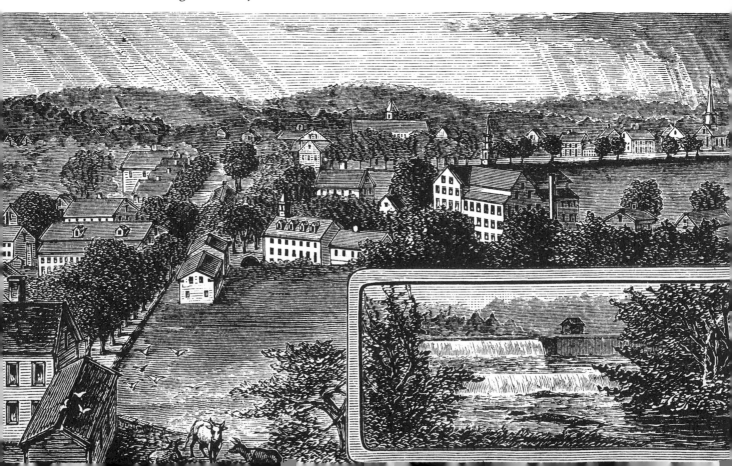

tablished a mill a few miles away and built a town around it. He named the town Slatersville, after himself. His partners were Samuel Slater, William Almy, and various Browns.

The Slaters, the Browns, and Almy were all in competition with one another. The fact that they were, nevertheless, willing to join together and build more and bigger cotton mills suggests that there was plenty of business to go around. In fact, by 1810 there were 87 cotton mills in New England. By 1815, the number was 165. Samuel Slater owned 7 of them, either by himself or with partners.

Slater was a fine mechanic and an excellent manager of machinery, but he was not a brilliant inventor. After 1800, advances in American cotton manufacturing were made elsewhere. His mills kept using water wheels when others were getting their power from Oliver Evans's improved steam engine. The Slater mills began using steam power only in 1828.

Still, Slater was a pioneer, and his adopted country rewarded him with fame and wealth. In 1817, he showed President James Monroe around the old Pawtucket mill. The mill had grown from 72 spindles to over 5,000, but the original spinning frame from 1790 was still working away.

A dozen years later, another president, Andrew Jackson, came to call. Slater was by then an invalid.

"I understand you taught us how to spin," the president said, "so as to rival Great Britain in her manufactures; you

Samuel Slater

set all these thousands of spindles to work."

Slater replied, "Yes, sir, I suppose that I gave out the psalm, and they have been singing to the tune ever since."

Samuel Slater died in 1835, rich and respected. He was worth the stupendous sum of $1,200,000. His real importance, however, is summed up by other figures. In 1790, the United States produced 2 million pounds of raw cotton, a tiny fraction of which went to Slater's 72 spindles. In 1835, when Slater died, almost 80 million pounds of cotton a year fed the 2 million spindles of American mills. Those mills produced $47 million worth of goods. In 1790, less than 1 percent of Americans lived in cities. In 1835, largely because of the industrial development that Slater helped to set in motion, the figure was 10 percent and rising. The United States was well on its way to becoming the industrial, urban nation that Alexander Hamilton had foreseen back in 1791.

3

"INFANT INDUSTRIES" GROW UP

Thanks in part to Slater's innovations, America's young industries began to boom in the early nineteenth century.

For any industry to succeed, six things are needed. The first is *capital*. Capital is the money used to get the industry started—to build and equip the factory and keep it running until its products bring in money.

The second is *labor*. Once a factory is built and machines are installed, labor—working men and women (and, back then, children)—is needed to operate the machinery.

The third is *raw materials*—natural products like cotton, wool, iron, oil, or wood that the industry turns into finished goods.

The fourth is a *market* for the industry's product—there must be enough

Traveling peddlers, like the one in the painting, brought manufactured goods to farm families.

people who have both a need for the product and the money to buy it.

Fifth, industry needs *transportation* to bring raw materials to the factory and to carry finished products to markets beyond the local area.

Finally, industry needs *energy* to keep its machines running.

If we keep these six requirements in mind, we can see why the American textile industry grew up when and where it did.

Most wealthy people in the northeastern states were merchants. They made money shipping raw materials and goods to and from Europe. Their success gave them ready cash to invest. In the South, on the other hand, rich people owned large plantations. Their wealth was in the form of land and slaves, not cash. In the South, Samuel Slater would most probably not have found a Moses Brown to provide the capital for a textile mill.

The cotton gin made big plantations like this one profitable.

Labor, too, was readily available in the Northeast, especially in New England. The population there was less scattered than elsewhere in the nation. More important, the climate and the rocky soil kept farms small. Children and young adults could be spared from farm chores to earn money in the nearby towns. Also, mill owners often paid high wages to attract workers. Traditionally, one son in a family inherited the farm; the other sons went elsewhere and began farming on their own. Now these surplus sons had another choice: they could go to town and find work in the mills. But in many cases it was the daughters in farm families who first entered the mills.

Cotton, the raw material for textile manufacturing, came from the southern states. The soil and climate in the South were ideal for growing cotton. In the first decades of the nineteenth century, plantations grew in the newer southern states, such as Alabama and Mississippi. As the demand from up north grew, plantation owners eagerly planted acres and acres of cotton. The cotton plantations and the textile mills were as much as a thousand miles apart—but both were located near the ocean or on major rivers, and transportation by sea was easy and cheap.

There was a market for Slater's product: the 500,000 households in the United States. Each was a potential customer, if the price was low enough. Soon, the textile industry was like a dog chasing its tail: as the price went down, demand went up, because more people could afford the product. To meet this rising demand (*demand* means people's desire for goods), manufacturers made their mills larger and more efficient, which brought the price still lower, which created more demand, and so on.

Transportation was American industry's weak link in 1790. Sea transport up and down the Atlantic coast was easy, as we have seen. Transportation overland was another story. Outside the five biggest cities, there were no paved roads at all. Between cities and towns, a few roads were good enough to carry stagecoaches and mail carriers. Most roads, especially into the interior of the country, were no more than footpaths. Farmers who settled in the Ohio River valley after 1800 had to ship their products to the eastern cities the long way around: they sent them on flatboats down the Ohio and Mississippi rivers to New Orleans. There they were transferred to sailing ships for the long trip around Florida and then northward up the Atlantic coast. The whole trip took three to four months. But more and more people—all of them potential customers for America's new industries—were moving west of the Appalachian Mountains. Transportation had to be made faster, easier, and cheaper if these people were to benefit from America's young industries.

Before the steamboat, slow-moving flatboats like the one shown brought produce to market.

Slaves using a cotton gin.

For energy to run factories, New England had more swiftly flowing rivers than other parts of the country. Water wheels harnessed the power of running water, using it to run the machinery that first spun cotton, then later made cloth, shoes, guns, and everything from watches to locomotives.

New England, then, had everything industry needed: capital, water power, plenty of labor, and access to sea transport for bringing in raw materials and sending out finished goods to a wide market.

The cotton industry that Samuel Slater founded might not have grown as quickly as it did if a new method for processing raw cotton hadn't been developed in the 1790s.

In 1792, Eli Whitney, a Connecticut Yankee fresh out of Yale College, visited the Georgia plantation of Catherine Littlefield Greene. Whitney and Greene saw slaves slowly picking the seeds from cotton. Mrs. Greene suggested to Whitney that such a time-consuming, boring job could be done by machines. She also proposed some ideas for a machine that would separate the seeds from the cotton. Back home in New Haven, Whitney built a working model of such a machine, which he called a cotton gin, in ten days. (*Gin* was an early form of the word *engine*.) In April 1793, he produced his first full-size gin. Soon he had a factory turning out gin after gin, but he was unable to keep up with the demand. Every plantation in the South, it seemed, wanted a gin.

Whitney was delighted that the slaves no longer had to separate the seeds from the cotton by hand. He thought the invention would make life easier for them. In fact, it did not work out that way. Using the cotton gin, two slaves did the work that two dozen had done before. This made more slaves available for the backbreaking work in the cotton fields, so their masters could raise and sell more cotton to meet the growing demand from the northern mills. Again, we can see the dog chasing its tail: Slater's mill needed more and more raw cotton, which meant the cotton planters needed more and more of Whitney's cotton gins. Everyone benefited—except the slaves. They now had to work longer and harder hours in the fields. (Also, mill workers had to endure longer hours as the supply of cotton and the demand for cloth grew.) To make matters worse, as the plantations grew larger, one owner could no longer attend to everything. Planters began to employ overseers to supervise the slaves. These men (many of them northerners) were, as a rule, far harder on the slaves than the planters had been.

Slater's cotton mill inspired other industries, directly or indirectly. In 1794, the Schofield brothers emigrated from England and began producing cloth by water power.

As industry grew, the demand for machinery grew with it. By 1798, Slater's brother-in-law, David Wilkinson, was building machines full-time in his new water-powered mill in Pawtucket. In 1798, he patented the sliding lathe (a machine that made precise parts for other machines), the first of many tools he and other mechanics developed.

Oliver Evans, improver of the flour mill and the steam engine, developed machinery that made the iron teeth for carding machines at the amazing rate of 1,500 an hour.

By 1800, the use of water-powered machines had spread to other products, and new techniques were meeting new needs. But there was a problem. Formerly, manufactured goods were handmade by independent artisans, one item at a time. This method produced goods of excellent quality, but it was a slow process. Production could be increased and simplified if machine tools made large quantities of parts. The parts could then be assembled into finished products by less-skilled workers.

The first *interchangeable parts*, as they are called, were used by mechanics at the U.S. Arsenal in Springfield, Massachusetts. The arsenal workers used the parts to produce inexpensive, standardized guns for the American army. Because the parts were interchangeable, a part of one gun could easily fit into another. Eli Whitney gave a boost to the use of interchangeable parts in 1798. Whitney had received a government contract to make 10,000 rifles. To show the efficiency of the new manufacturing methods, he put on a clever demonstration. From ten piles of parts, he put together ten rifles, proving that any of the parts would fit perfectly in any of the weapons. Whitney's demonstration convinced many in the United States that interchangeable parts made complicated mechanisms cheaper and easier to produce.

At first, this technique was used mostly to make firearms. In the 1820s, Simeon North applied it to clocks, which had always been expensive luxuries. Mass production using interchangeable parts made them available to many homes. Cyrus McCormick invented a harvesting machine in 1831, and by the 1840s he was mass-producing his reaper (a machine that *reaps*, or harvests, grain) from interchangeable parts. His machines sold

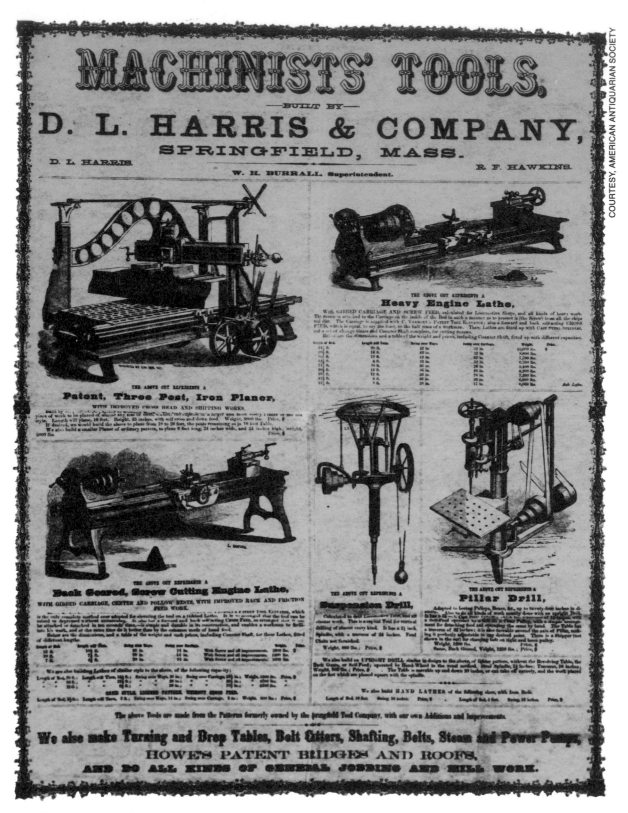

Machine tools—tools that make other tools—played an important part in American industrialization.

well because with a reaper, one family could maintain a farm much larger than the traditional forty acres of pre-industrial times.

Not all of these developments met with praise. The rise in manufacturing put many independent artisans and their families out of work. To a master gunsmith, the idea of a machine stamping out musket parts was threatening. Artisans spent years learning their crafts and many more years perfecting their skills. Now an untrained worker using a machine could produce more guns in a week than a gunsmith could in months. To the artisan—and to many farmers—industrialization meant the end of a hard but cherished way of life. They feared that the "republican virtues" of independence and self-sufficiency were fast disappearing from the United States.

New ideas and techniques also appeared in the textile industry. For years, the cotton that was spun by machine had to be woven into cloth by hand on small, slow looms. Then, in 1813, Francis Cabot Lowell, a Boston businessman, and a mechanic named Paul Moody built a power loom. The new machine used water power to weave cloth automatically from cotton yarn. Lowell based his loom on ones he had seen on a visit to England.

Like Slater's spinning machinery before it, the power loom made finished goods faster and cheaper than handwork. Lowell, however, was more ambitious than Slater. He wanted to put the whole process of making cloth

Eli Whitney

under one roof. His mills would card, draw, spin, and weave the cotton, then bleach it and print colored designs on it. Beyond that, Lowell wanted to produce his goods in huge quantities. This meant he would need bigger buildings and more machines—and therefore more capital than he and a few other men could put up.

Lowell tried a new kind of business organization: a *joint stock company*. He founded the Boston Manufacturing Company and sold *shares* of stock in the

An 1883 advertisement shows the testing of the first McCormick reaper in 1831.

company to anyone who had money to invest. Each shareholder owned a piece of the business and was entitled to part of the profits.

Suppose a company issued a thousand shares of stock at $100 each. An investor with $1,000 to spend could buy ten shares. Then the investor would "own" one one-hundredth, or 1 percent, of the company and would be entitled to 1 percent of any profits it made. Shareholders could keep the shares and collect *dividends*—their portion of the profits. Or the shares could be sold.

If the company turned out to be profitable, the value of its stock rose *above*

par—the original purchase price. Suppose the company in our example did well and began paying big dividends. The shares would go up in value, and the original investor could sell them at a profit. Other investors would be eager to buy, either to collect the dividends or in the hope that the value of the shares would keep rising.

If the company did poorly and could not pay dividends, the value of the shares dropped—went *below par*. The investor had gambled on the new company and lost, but he or she wasn't stuck. The investor could sell the shares for less than the price they had been paid for, recovering at least part of the investment. Who would buy them? Another investor, one who was willing to gamble that the company's business would improve.

The joint stock company made it easier for new industries to raise money. Many people, not just two or three partners, put up the money. This made more cash available, and it spread out the risk of losses if the company should fail.

To those who profited, the joint stock company was a wonderful innovation. Not all Americans felt that way. Those who held the "Jeffersonian" view pointed out that most Americans had always lived off what their farms or workshops produced. Someone who profited from stock ventures, however, lived off money. In other words, the joint-stock investor really didn't *produce* anything—at least not with his or her own hands. To some, this was a betrayal of the simple republican values that Jefferson and his followers cherished. Followers of Hamilton, however, argued that joint-stock ventures fueled new enterprises and industries from which all Americans would eventually benefit.

By selling stock to well-to-do Bostonians, Lowell raised over $400,000 to finance his new textile business. The company built a large group of mill buildings in Waltham, Massachusetts, near Boston. In its first year, the firm had sales of only $3,000. Three years later, in 1817, sales were $300,000, and the people who had bought stock were happily counting their 20 percent dividends.

By 1823, business was so good that Lowell and his associates were ready to expand. They needed room for even more mills and machines. They set up a new firm, the Merrimack Manufacturing Company, with capital stock worth over $600,000. Their agents went to farmers on the Merrimack River northwest of Boston and bought their land cheaply, sometimes by lying—telling the farmers that the land would be used to raise fruit and sheep. This unfair way of getting inexpensive land angered farmers. Many farmers in New England saw the clanking, unfamiliar mills as a threat to their way of life. Occasionally, farmers attempted to burn the new mills down. The same thing had happened on a large scale in England, which had gone through major industrial changes sixty years before. Bands of "Luddites" (named for their leader, Ned Ludd) had smashed the looms and burned the mills that were quickly putting cloth weavers out of work. In a famous poem, the poet William Blake had protested the "dark satanic mills" that were appearing in the green countryside of England. Now similar mills were rising along the riverbanks of New England.

But the Lowell Company soon had the land it needed, and enormous mills went up in the new city of Lowell on the banks of the Merrimack. Other textile companies built there as well. By 1836, the mills in the city were worth over $6 million and employed 6,800 workers.

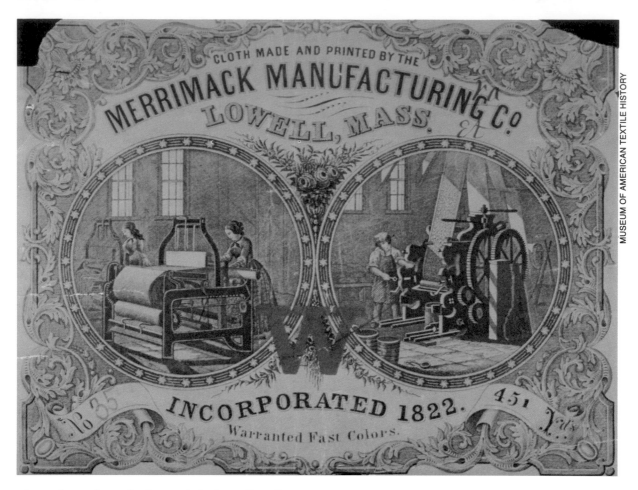

An early trademark of one of the Lowell mills.

Now that cloth was spun and woven by machinery, many believed that a machine for sewing it was the next logical step. Many mechanics tried and failed to build such a machine. In the 1830s, Walter Hunt solved the basic problem by moving the eye of the needle down to the sharp end. He never patented or developed his machine, however, because he was afraid it would put seamstresses out of work. Hunt had realized something that other early industrialists didn't, or chose to ignore—the fact that new techniques rarely benefit everyone. For every advance in manufacturing, some people were thrown out of work or off their land.

Elias Howe, a Boston watchmaker, was less thoughtful. In 1845, he demonstrated a practical sewing machine based on Hunt's ideas. Howe proved that his machine could outproduce five seamstresses. It was slow to catch on, but by 1850 he and several imitators were successfully using interchangeable parts to mass-produce sewing machines. Now an American housewife could buy cloth spun and woven by machine and sew it into clothing in a fraction of the time it would take her by hand. Or she could buy clothes ready-made, in factories equipped with the same mass-produced sewing machines.

Beefed up, Howe's machine could sew leather as well as cloth—and so shoemaking left the local cobbler's shop and went to factories that mass-produced shoes for sale over a wide area.

The term *Industrial Revolution* is often used to describe the development of manufacturing from 1790 to around 1850. The word *revolution* suggests a sudden overturn, like the seven-year war that freed the colonies from English rule. It is important to remember that the Industrial Revolution lasted sixty years—a person's lifetime in those days. This revolution didn't just change the way goods were made. It changed American society.

The Industrial Revolution created a new class—wage earners. Before industrialization, almost all Americans ate the food they raised themselves or bought with the proceeds of their small workshops. Now many Americans received wages for factory work. While many workers liked the new system—factory work was hard, but so was farming—there were drawbacks. The farm family rarely had much money, but they usually had enough food and a roof over their heads, even in hard times. If hard times hit a working family, however, great hardship could result. There was no social security, health insurance, or other such benefits in those days. A worker who became too sick or old to

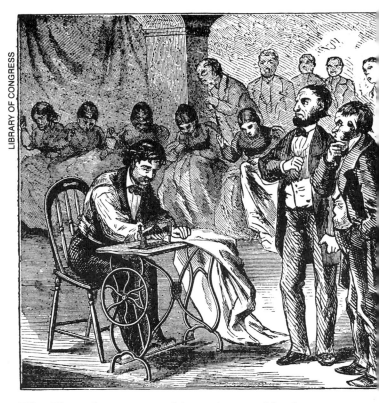

Elias Howe demonstrates his sewing machine by having it race five seamstresses.

work simply lost his or her job, whether or not a family depended on his or her wages. The result was usually poverty. Even Samuel Slater had realized this harsh fact. When President Andrew Jackson visited Slater in 1840, Jackson told him he was glad that Slater and his family had grown rich from his mills. Slater replied, "So am I glad to know it, for I should not like to be a pauper [poor person] in this country, where they are put up to auction to the lowest bidder."

Unemployment also happened when business was bad. Despite the industrial boom of the nineteenth century, prosperity was never continuous. Sometimes, joint-stock investors lost confidence and stopped investing money in the new industries, or economic conditions at home or overseas led to a drop in demand. This situation was called a *panic*. One such panic took place in 1819, when a flood of cheap British goods drove many American manufacturers out of business. A year later, Senator Henry Clay told Congress what he saw on a visit to New England: "Large buildings, with the glass knocked out of the windows, enveloped in solitary gloom. Upon inquiry, you are almost always informed that they were some cotton or other factory." The economy eventually recovered, but panics and depressions occurred from time to time for the rest of the century—and into our own time.

There was another series of changes that went hand in hand with the Industrial Revolution: the revolution in transportation.

In 1790, there were no surfaced roads in the United States, except a few close to big cities. Raw materials and finished goods moved, when they moved at all, by ships going up and down the coast, by flatboats floating down the rivers, and by ox-drawn carts on the winding, rutted dirt roads.

But it was not just the developing industries that needed better transportation. Americans were on the move, heading west.

During the years of English rule, the rich lands west of the Appalachian Mountains were off limits to settlers. The English did not care to spend money protecting settlers from Native Americans, who were defending their own way of life. After the Revolutionary War, the dam broke, and people flooded into the territory between the Appalachians and the Mississippi River. Land there was cheap, and there was enough for those who wanted to move west.

Once an area had a population of 60,000, it could petition Congress for statehood. The dates the states were admitted to the Union tell the story of settlement: Kentucky, 1792; Tennessee, 1796; Ohio, 1803; Louisiana, 1812; Indiana, 1816; Mississippi, 1817; Illinois, 1818. What had been a wilderness in 1790 was, by 1820, settled with farmers, some of whom had products to sell and money to spend on manufactured goods.

The first major improvement in transportation was the National Road, approved by Congress in 1806, started in 1811 at Cumberland, Maryland, and built across the Appalachians to the Ohio River at Wheeling, Virginia, by 1818. Eventually the road stretched all the way to Vandalia, Illinois, along the route now followed by U.S. Highway 40.

Other east-west roads were built by state governments or private turnpike companies. By 1820, improved roads connected Albany and Buffalo, New York; Philadelphia and Pittsburgh, Pennsylvania; and other key cities. The roads were often impassable because of snow, flooding, or mud. These "corduroy roads" were paved with logs. Still, they were better than the trails they replaced. They opened new markets and

Pioneers like Daniel Boone, shown above leading settlers to Kentucky, helped open up the American West.

new sources of raw materials to the growing industries in the East.

River transportation, too, improved after 1800. Many experimenters had tried to combine the steam engine and the boat into a method of transportation that did not rely on wind or human muscle power. In fact, a man named John Fitch had demonstrated a steamboat in Philadelphia during the Constitutional Convention in 1787. It wasn't until 1807, however, that a practical steamboat was put into constant use. That vessel was the *Clermont*, and it was developed by Robert Fulton.

Robert Fulton, with Clermont *in the background.*

Like Samuel Slater and Eli Whitney, Robert Fulton was a forward-thinking person of many talents. He had been a gunsmith, a painter, and a ship designer before he turned his attention to steam power. In 1807, Hudson's steamboat chugged up the Hudson River from New York City to Albany. The *Clermont* covered the distance of almost 150 miles in 32 hours. In 1811, the first steamboats were navigating the Ohio River. Steamboats were fast and reliable (usually, although crude boilers sometimes exploded). Best of all, they didn't depend on the wind or human or animal power.

On the Ohio-Mississippi river system, steamboats made the 1,500-mile trip from Louisville to New Orleans in seven days; the return trip, upriver, in sixteen days. Transporting goods by steamboat cost one-tenth what it had cost by flatboat, which took a month to make the same trip downstream and three months to come back up. By 1840, 536 steamboats hauled freight and passengers on the Mississippi. Even earlier, in 1819, sailing ships assisted by steam had begun traveling back and forth across the Atlantic Ocean.

Steamboats made long-distance transportation faster and cheaper, but they could go only where there were rivers, and up those rivers only as far as the first falls. The solution was to "build rivers" where they were needed, by digging canals.

Several short, local canals already existed when New York's governor DeWitt Clinton proposed digging a canal 350 miles from Albany, on the Hudson River, to Buffalo, on Lake Erie. The digging started in 1817, and the canal was finished in 1825. Thousands of laborers worked on the project. Many of these canal diggers were immigrants from Europe, especially Ireland. The canal cost $7 million to build; in the first year of operation it earned $700,000, and in seven years it had paid for itself.

Again, a new mode of transportation made it cheaper and faster to move goods. The trip from Buffalo to New York City now took six days instead of twenty; the cost of moving a ton of freight one mile dropped from 20 cents to 2 cents. Farmers in Ohio no longer had to ship their produce down the river to New Orleans and then up the coast to New York or Boston. Steamboats and canal boats gave these western farmers a cheaper, faster, more direct route.

In 1828, a load of lumber traveled 900 miles from the forests of Michigan to Worcester, Massachusetts, entirely by water. (It could have gone on to Pawtucket, by the newly built Blackstone Canal.)

Soon the Erie Canal had its imitators: dozens of canals were planned, started, sometimes even finished in a great "canal boom" between 1825 and 1835. Every state, it seemed, wanted its own canal and the economic benefits it would bring. Unfortunately, many canal planners ignored geography. The Erie Canal was easy to build and maintain because it crossed flat country. A similar canal across the rugged mountains of

Boats carrying freight and passengers ply the newly completed Erie Canal.

Pennsylvania from Philadelphia to Pittsburgh was an economic and engineering disaster. Only a few canals got past the planning stage.

Ten years after the Erie Canal opened, canals were on their way to becoming obsolete. Americans were excited about a new transportation miracle: the railroad.

Wagons pulled by horses had traveled on tracks for years, usually carrying coal or iron ore from mines to nearby rivers. And inventors had long tried to use steam power to move land vehicles. In 1782, for example, Oliver

Evans developed a "steam carriage," which he was never able to perfect. The Englishman Richard Trevthick built a successful steam locomotive in 1801, and in 1825 the world's first steam railroad began making regular trips in England.

The United States was not far behind. In 1829, the Delaware & Hudson Canal Company bought two locomotives from England. In 1830, the first American-built engine, Peter Cooper's Tom Thumb, made an experimental run on the then horse-drawn Baltimore & Ohio Railroad. Later that year, The Best

In 1830, Peter Cooper's Tom Thumb *locomotive raced a horse. The horse won when the locomotive broke down.*

Friend of Charleston went into regular service on the Charleston & Hamburg Railroad in South Carolina. Railroads had arrived.

By 1840, the United States had 3,000 miles of railroads. Ten years later, the mileage had jumped to 79,000, and canals were a thing of the past.

Like canals, steamboats, and roads before them, railroads made transportation cheaper. Freight charges on the Baltimore & Ohio were a fourth of those on the competing turnpikes. With the coming of railroads to Massachusetts, the cost of shipping goods from Boston to Worcester dropped 66 percent.

Besides being cheap, railroad transportation was convenient. Rails could be laid anywhere—across flat country, in tunnels dug through mountains, on bridges across rivers. Trains stopped anywhere there was freight to drop off or pick up.

Railroads were built where the business was. Starting in the thickly populated industrial areas of the East, they spread westward into the farmlands of the Ohio and Mississippi valleys. Now farmers had a better way than ever to ship food to the growing cities of the Atlantic coast. Manufacturers had easy access to customers hundreds and thousands of miles away from their factories.

Besides helping trade and manufacturing with faster, cheaper transportation, railroads brought growth in related industries. The iron industry grew as huge quantities of iron were needed for rails, car wheels, and locomotives. To make iron took iron ore and coal, so mining companies developed new tools and techniques to increase production. Because trains had to run on exact schedules, the growth of railroads even brought growth in the mass production of inexpensive pocket watches. Less directly, by making farming more profitable through lower costs and by opening up new land to farming, railroads boosted the sales of mass-produced farm equipment.

But as always, industrial growth brought problems as well as benefits. Just as the sewing machine put seamstresses out of work, the railroad led to unemployment among people who depended on road- or canalside taverns, inns, and stables for a living. There was a second group of people, wealthier than the first, who also opposed the railroads. They were those who had invested heavily in the canal industry. The railroad boom put a swift end to the canal boom. Investors watched their stock drop in value as the freight and passengers abandoned the canals for the faster, more efficient railroads.

But the railroads were here to stay, along with mills, factories, steamboats, and all the good and bad things the Industrial Revolution had brought to the young United States. If the farmers we met in the first chapter were around as the United States neared the halfway mark of the nineteenth century, they would have to admit that Hamilton's viewpoint, not Jefferson's, now ruled the American scene. Although not all of its citizens were happy with the results of industrialization, the United States was well on its way to becoming a society of industrial workers.

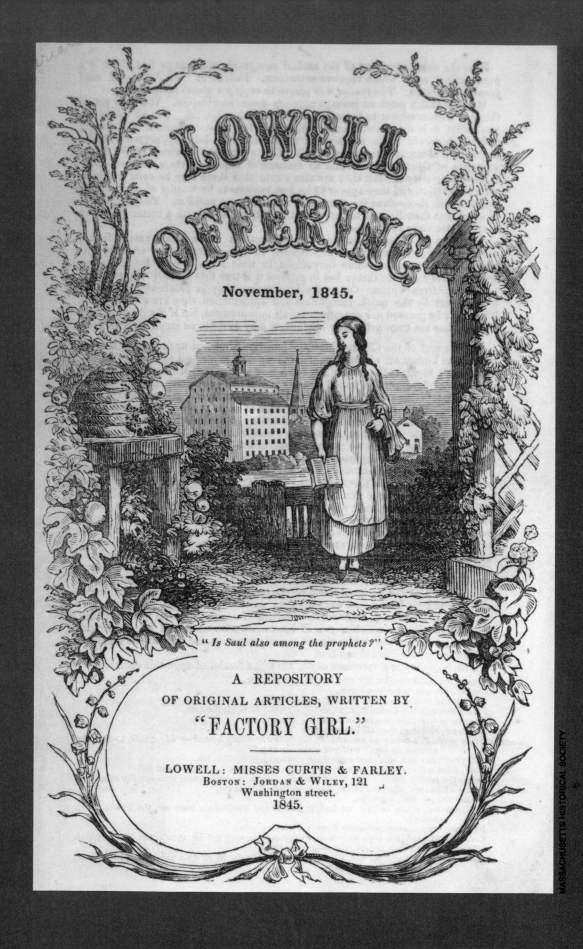

LOWELL OFFERING

November, 1845.

"*Is Saul also among the prophets?*"

A REPOSITORY
OF ORIGINAL ARTICLES, WRITTEN BY
"FACTORY GIRL."

LOWELL: MISSES CURTIS & FARLEY.
BOSTON: JORDAN & WILEY, 121
Washington street.
1845.

4

WORKING IN THE MILL

The nine children who went to work for Samuel Slater in the winter of 1790 were among the first of a new kind of American: the factory worker.

To us, the idea of small children working all day in a noisy mill seems strange, even brutal. Today, the law says children under sixteen or eighteen can work only in certain jobs. The hours they can work are limited. In most states, those under fourteen cannot work at all. Other laws require that people attend school until the age of sixteen.

But two hundred years ago, things were different. On the farm, where most Americans lived, a child had to help with the work as much as he or she was able. And it was *work*—not just milking a cow or picking berries. Before the coming of labor-saving machinery,

The title page of the November 1845 Lowell Offering.

farm work was even longer and more backbreaking than it is today. This was especially so in the spring, when land was plowed and crops were planted, and in the fall, when crops were harvested. Without plenty of children to work, a farm might not succeed.

Children in villages and towns worked, too, unless they were born into wealthy families. A boy either learned his father's trade, by working beside him, or became an apprentice, as Samuel Slater did back in England. The apprentice agreed to live in his master's house for seven years. He was given food, clothing, and shelter—but no pay. Working with the master, the apprentice learned the skills and secrets of his chosen trade. At the end of the apprenticeship, at around age twenty-one, he was a *journeyman*, qualified to sell his labor and, if he could save up enough money, set up his own shop. Later, with his own shop, he could have apprentices who worked for him.

If the apprentice was lucky, he went into partnership with his master. If he was unlucky—if the master beat him, or starved him, or loaded him down with dirty work instead of teaching him the trade—the apprentice was stuck. Often, his only choice was to run away—as Benjamin Franklin did when he was seventeen.

Some girls were apprenticed as servants. In cities, girls sometimes signed seven-year apprentice contracts. They received training in the skills of housekeeping or, sometimes, sewing. However, most girls were not apprenticed. Their usual role was to stay at home and help their mothers run the house. In premachine days, housekeeping, like farming, was harder work than it is today. By the age of five or six, a girl was expected to help with the unskilled work of the household, like churning butter, scrubbing clothes, and peeling vegetables. As she grew older, she learned cooking, sewing, spinning, and other skills. She might also tend the family garden and do work for the church. The workdays were long.

If a family had more daughters than they needed to keep the home running, a girl might be "hired out"—sent to another family as a paid servant. Her life was like that of an apprentice, but the money she earned was given to her parents.

The skills that most girls learned were useful for only one job: that of wife and mother. Only a few other occupations were open to them. An unmarried woman could make her living on her own as a seamstress, sewing clothes ordered by others; by doing embroidery and other needlework; or by painting decorations on plates and dishes. Some single women opened elementary schools, called "dame schools." Some gave lessons in music, painting, and other arts. Others helped their artisan husbands with their work. If the husband died, his widow might take over his workshop.

Children working in mills and factories was something new, however. On a farm, a child worked with his or her family. In a workshop, an apprentice worked closely with a craftsman. But in a mill, a child worked not with his or her family, or even a trusted artisan. The child worker tended a machine, and the machinery at Slater's first mill ran well into the night. Many parents objected when Slater wanted their children to work at night.

But Slater was not a cruel boss. He felt he was responsible for his workers' well-being. After all, one of them was his brother-in-law. Slater opened a school for the children, where they learned reading, writing, and arithmetic. At first, Slater himself taught the children. Later, as the expanding business took more and more of his time, he handed the teaching over to students from nearby Brown University.

In a time when there was no public education, the school was an important extra for the young factory workers. They may not have appreciated it, though. School met on Sunday, their only full day off.

Children at work in a New England textile mill.

The other days, they worked—from 5:30 in the morning until 7:30 at night Monday through Friday, and from early morning into the afternoon on Saturday. In the winter, hours were shorter, sunrise to sunset. These children had little time or energy left for play.

The mill was not a pleasant place to work. The machinery made a deafening racket. Cotton dust filled the air, making throats and nostrils itch and burn. In the winter, a few stoves barely warmed the room. In the summer, the heat was unbearable because the windows had to be kept shut or cool breezes would blow the raw cotton around.

The children were needed for their agility, not their muscle power. Older boys and men did the heavy lifting. Usually, a child working in Slater's mill did not work fourteen straight hours every day. Machinery often had to be adjusted, repaired, or reloaded. During these interruptions, the young workers were free to leave their machines and amuse themselves.

Pay for child workers was low: 12½ to 25 cents per day. The amount seems tiny today, but two hundred years ago it made an important contribution to the family's income.

Some people worried about child labor. Josiah Quincy, a Quaker, visited

47

one of Slater's mills in 1801. He felt pity for "these little creatures, plying [working] in a contracted [crowded] room, among flyers and coggs, at an age when nature requires for them air, space, and sports. There was a dull dejection in the countenances [faces] of all of them."

As the textile industry grew in Pawtucket and nearby towns, a pattern called the Rhode Island system developed. Mills hired entire families. The younger children tended the drawing and spinning machinery while older children and adults did other work around the mill. When mill owners needed more workers, they advertised in the newspapers—not for individuals but for families. Families with many children were the most desirable.

As new mills were built, the owners built workers' housing, stores, even schools and churches along with them. The families that worked in the mill had their rent taken out of their pay. Some owners paid them in *scrip*—"private money" that they could spend only at the company store.

Today, some people say the mill owners built houses and stores for their workers only to make money by taking back some of their already low pay. Others point out that the owners had to provide housing and shopping if they wanted to attract workers.

And the workers came. Despite long hours and low pay, they could make good money working in the mills, compared with that made by other workers. An average mill family in the early 1800s could make $658 a year. The same family, staying on the farm and raising most of their own food, made the equivalent of $180 a year.

Of course, a mill family had to pay rent and buy food with their wages, while the farm family usually owned their own land and raised their own food. Also, a farm family could get things it needed through *barter*—trading for products or services instead of using money. A family of mill workers had to pay cash when clothes or food were needed. Still, mill workers could save money from their wages—unless a factory layoff or an illness in the family made them use up their savings.

The mill also offered opportunity—at least to males. A bright, observant boy tending a spinning frame could hope to work his way up to more skilled work. He might become a mechanic, earning high pay—well over a dollar a day—for repairing the complex machinery and keeping it running.

The mills, however, were no paradise for workers, especially young workers. In 1820, more than half the workers in Rhode Island textile mills were children fourteen or younger. By then, the day when small mills were managed by their owners was over. Slater and other owners no longer managed their mills personally. The day-to-day running of mills was done by overseers. The courts saw overseers as substitute parents, with the same power to punish children as their natural parents. In 1823, an overseer was put on trial for beating a young girl employee. He was let off because of the substitute-parent

Mill workers prepare cotton for spinning.

principle. In 1831, a boy who ran away from the mill where he worked was flogged by the overseer. Abuses like these were probably not common, but they did happen, especially if the child worker did not have older family members working with him or her in the mill.

Life in the mills took some getting used to. Children had to learn new habits. On the farm, a family did different things at different times of the year. In the autumn, a child might spend all day helping to bring in a harvest. In the spring, he or she would help with the planting. But in the mill, the child worker did the same thing day in and out. It didn't matter if it was raining, or if it was the middle of the winter—the machinery kept working, and so did the worker. People raised on farms, where life changed with the seasons, had to adjust to this new way of work. Some workers grumbled that instead of running the machines, the machines were running the people.

North of Rhode Island, in the huge new mills of Lowell, Massachusetts, a different pattern of work came into being. The Lowell system, as it was called, did not depend on families all working in the mill. Some young children worked in the Lowell factories, but most of Lowell's workers were older. The typical Lowell worker was a woman in her late teens or early twenties. She lived away from home, on her own, and she made her own money.

By 1836, the mills in and around Lowell had 6,000 workers—85 percent

Workers head home after a long day in a New England mill in this engraving by Winslow Homer.

of them women aged fifteen to thirty. These "Lowell Girls" made $6 to $10 a week, which was good pay.

The idea of a young woman leaving home and making her way in the world was shocking to many people. Young women, they believed, shouldn't work for wages. A girl was supposed to stay at home, helping her mother and obeying her father, and someday marry—with her family's approval—a farmer's son from their hometown. If a girl had to work, some people thought, she should work as a servant, not as a mill hand.

The mill owners took steps to make their new idea acceptable. They built large dormitories for their workers and charged $1.25 a week rent. The bathrooms were out back away from the dormitories. There was no running water.

Older women of good character managed the dormitories. They enforced strict rules. Everyone had to be in bed by ten o'clock. No liquor was allowed in company housing. Church attendance was required. A girl could have male visitors, but only in the downstairs parlor under the watchful eye of the manager.

The Lowell system worked. Young women flocked to the mills from the farms and country towns of Massachusetts, New Hampshire, and Vermont. Most of them came not to escape poverty back home but to improve themselves in some way. A Vermont girl named Mary Paul wrote to her father: "I am in need of clothes which I cannot get about here and for that reason I want to go to Lowell or some other place."

Many of the mill workers wanted to

be independent. One wrote home: "I have but one life to live and I want to enjoy myself as well as I can while I live."

Others saw factory work as a way to better things. A Lowell worker named Lucy Ann wrote to a friend in 1851: "I have earned enough to school me awhile, and have not I a right to do so, or must I go home, like a dutiful girl, place the money in father's hands, and then there goes all my hard earnings." Instead of going home, Lucy Ann went from the Lowell mills to Oberlin College in Ohio, one of the few colleges in the United States that accepted women.

Many suffered from homesickness at first, but most enjoyed their independence and their earning power. For some of them, home lost much of its charm. The Currer sisters, back home in Wentworth, Massachusetts, for a visit, wrote to a friend in Lowell: "It is extremely dull here now, there is nothing at all interesting going on here."

Working in Lowell showed the young women a wider world and gave them the money to enjoy it. They bought fashionable clothes, but they also bought books and magazines, paid for education, and joined a variety of social clubs, church groups, and reading and discussion circles. Most managed their income well. More than half put money in the Lowell Institution for Savings. The women workers of Lowell even published their own magazine in the 1840s. *The Lowell Offering*, the first American magazine produced entirely by women, contained stories, poems, and essays, as well as valuable descriptions of life in the mills.

"Mill girls" work a power loom in a Lowell mill.

MUSEUM OF AMERICAN TEXTILE HISTORY

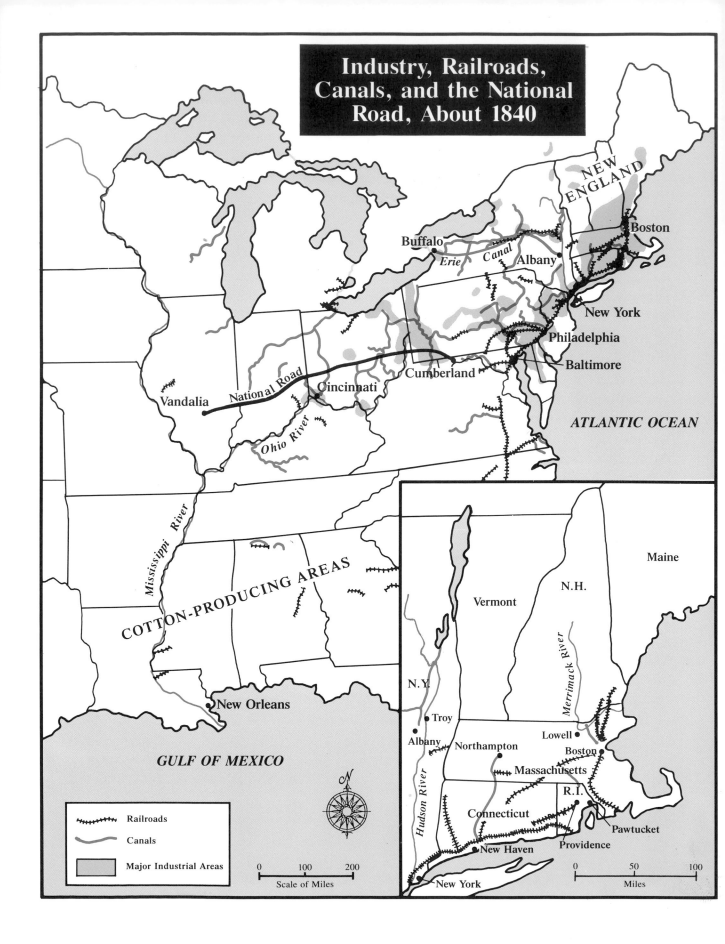

Industry, Railroads, Canals, and the National Road, About 1840

NEW ENGLAND

Buffalo

Erie *Canal*

Albany

Boston

New York

Philadelphia

Baltimore

Cumberland

Vandalia

National Road

Cincinnati

Ohio River

Mississippi River

COTTON-PRODUCING AREAS

New Orleans

ATLANTIC OCEAN

GULF OF MEXICO

N

Railroads

Canals

Major Industrial Areas

0   100   200
Scale of Miles

Inset map (New England)

Maine

Vermont

N.H.

N.Y.

Merrimack River

Troy

Albany

Northampton

Lowell

Boston

Massachusetts

Hudson River

R.I.

Connecticut

Pawtucket

New Haven

Providence

New York

0   50   100
Miles

Going to work in Lowell did not mean a life sentence of drudgery in the mills. The turnover of workers was high. The women usually contracted to work in one mill for a year, but most changed jobs more often than that. Overall, most of the women worked two or three years, with breaks for school or visits home. Then most would marry—but not necessarily the farm boy next door. A writer of the time said the mill workers "will nine times out of ten, marry a mechanic instead of a farmer. They know that marrying a farmer is a serious business. They remember their worn-out mothers."

The most important thing the Lowell system gave its young female workers was *choice*. For the first time, a woman could choose how to make her money and how to spend it. She could choose her friends and even her husband from a growing city, instead of a country town. She could choose her religion—Lowell had a dozen different churches. Opportunities for women were still limited, but she could choose her future in a way her mother and grandmother would never have dreamed possible. It is fair to say that for some women, the mills of Lowell were the first step out of the farmhouse kitchen.

In the early years of America's Industrial Revolution, economic success came fairly easily. As demand for their products increased, the mills grew in size and number. The money rolled in, and there were jobs for almost anyone who wanted to work. Mills could not run without workers, so the owners usually treated their workers well, and paid them well (by the standards of the day).

But business has its ups and downs. In the early 1800s, there were frequent slumps—periods when business was slow, manufacturing costs were up, and prices were down. The mill owner's first move at such times was to save money by lowering the workers' pay. The workers learned that their best answer was to refuse to work when wages were cut. This meant going on strike.

The first recorded strike in an American factory was at one of Samuel Slater's mills in Pawtucket in 1824. When their workday was made an hour longer and their pay was cut 25 percent, the workers held meetings and protest marches and then went on strike. The owners could not afford to have the mill standing empty, so they gave in to the workers' demands.

In the bigger mills of Massachusetts, the workers had a harder time putting pressure on the owners. These mill owners had enough money in the bank to sit out strikes. They could afford to have their factories idle. More important, the owners always worked together: if one mill cut the workers' pay, all the others did the same. Pay for workers stopped when they were on strike, but the workers' rent had to be paid and food had to be bought.

The workers tried to use the same methods against mill owners who cut their pay. In 1834, 800 women from several mills walked off the job over a cut in pay. The men who owned the mills were shocked by this action. The mill owners held their ground, and the strike failed. The women went back to work at the reduced wages.

But the women had learned a lesson. Two years later, the owners tried to raise the rent in company housing. This time, 2,000 workers, a third of the city's work force, went on strike. The strikers were better organized, and this time it was the owners who had to give in.

In the early 1800s, unhappy workers could simply find another mill or factory, or perhaps return to the farm. But as the nineteenth century went on, these options grew less and less practical. Industrial workers realized that they would have to *organize* themselves if they wanted better treatment from their employers.

The early New England strikes showed that working people had power when they acted together. Beginning in the 1830s, workers tried to form labor unions to protect their common interests. The owners fought back. Workers who urged their fellow employees to join unions were fired, then blacklisted (put on a list of "troublemakers," which was circulated among mill owners) so that other mills would not hire them. The courts cooperated with employers by ruling that unions were illegal. Labor unions did not become powerful in mill towns until well after the Civil War ended in 1865.

The 1840s and 1850s were decades of reform in the United States. Americans started associations to battle every kind of evil, from slavery to drinking alcohol. Factory workers formed groups that called for labor reform in the form of new laws. They wanted shorter hours and better working conditions. They also wanted safe places to work—early mill machinery was unsafe. Accidents happened often, and some workers lost hands, eyes, or even their lives.

The main demand was for a ten-hour workday. Progress was slow. In Massachusetts, the ten-hour day for children working in factories became law in 1842. In Rhode Island, where a larger percentage of the work force was made up of children, the ten-hour day did not come until 1885.

By 1850, the American labor force had changed in another important way. More and more factory workers were immigrants. These new workers came to the United States to escape hunger and political turmoil in Europe. Because they were alone and friendless in their new country, mill owners found the immigrants easier to control. Native-born workers looked down on them as intruders who were willing to work for lower pay and afraid to stand up for their rights. Distrust between native-born and immigrant workers harmed American labor by making it hard for workers to unite against their bosses.

As the United States approached the halfway point of the nineteenth century, the nation, and its people, had come far. The majority of people still worked on farms. But those days when most Americans lived on farms and were self-supporting were fading into history. A new American society, a society of workers, was fast taking its place.

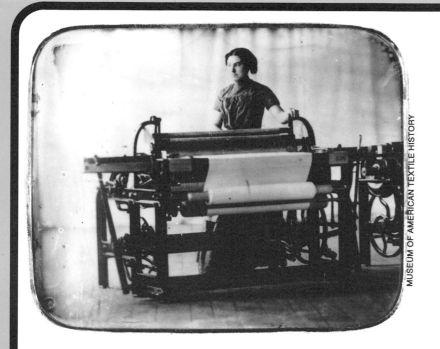

MUSEUM OF AMERICAN TEXTILE HISTORY

A STRIKE AT LOWELL

Many of the young women "operatives" at Lowell were happy to be earning money in the mills rather than eking out an existence on the farm. But from time to time, labor unrest broke out at Lowell. This usually happened when the mill owners tried to cut wages in order to raise profits. In October 1836, the mill owners made such an attempt. The mill girls responded by going on strike—or "turning out," as they called it. More than half a century later, a former operative recalled the event.

One of the girls stood on a pump, and gave vent to the feelings of her companions in a neat speech, declaring that it was their duty to resist all attempts at cutting down their wages. This was the first time a woman had spoken in public in Lowell. . . .

My own recollection of this first strike is very vivid. I had heard the first strike fully . . . discussed; I had been an ardent listener to what was said against this attempt at "oppression" on the part of the corporation, and naturally I took sides with the strikers.

When the day came on which the girls were to turn out, those in the upper rooms started first, and so many of them left that our mill was shut down. Then, when the girls in my room stood irresolute, uncertain what to do, asking each other, "Would you?" or "Shall we turn out?" and not one of them having the courage to lead off, I, who began to think they would not go out, after all their talk, became impatient, and started on ahead, saying, with childish bravado, "I don't care what you do, *I* am going to turn out, whether any one else does or not;" and I marched out and was followed by the others.

The operative who led her workers out on strike was only eleven years old at the time.

The 1836 strike failed, and wages were cut. They would be cut again. But the mill girls of Lowell had taken a bold step toward recognition of organized labor.

AFTERWORD

A CHANGED COUNTRY

A young woman who went to work in Samuel Slater's first mill back in 1790 would have been about seventy years old in 1850, had she lived that long. That woman lived in a United States that had changed in many ways—more ways, probably, than she realized.

The majority of Americans still lived on farms. But every year, more and more people left farms to live and work in cities and towns. More and more of the everyday things all Americans needed were made in factories, not by their own hands or in an artisan's shop nearby. Shoes, cloth, hats, pots and pans, rugs, blankets, furniture, tools, pistols and rifles, clocks, stoves, dishes—all these and more poured out of big factories where hundreds or thousands of workers mass-produced them with machines.

Steamboats brought prosperity to river towns like St. Louis, seen here about 1850.

The books and newspapers she read were printed by the tens of thousands on high-speed presses. Mail came to her quickly on fast trains. Urgent messages could be sent in seconds by the newfangled telegraph.

As a New Englander, she probably still lived in the Northeast. But her family was most probably spread over a large area. Children and grandchildren might live a thousand or more miles away, in the rich lands of the Mississippi valley or even in the new territories in the West.

Wherever her children and grandchildren lived, they might be farmers. If they were, they farmed in new and different ways. Steel plows, made in factories, broke up the soil. Mechanical reapers harvested the crops. Farmers could produce more food on bigger farms than in 1790. They no longer grew food just for their own use. They sold it; freight trains took it to the cities and towns, where it fed the factory workers.

By 1850, a network of railroads was tying the United States together.

But her children and grandchildren might well earn their living in other ways. They might be factory workers or managers; or merchants, selling the products of the factories; or clerks, bookkeepers, or bankers, making the growing business of the nation run smoothly. They might work at jobs nobody in 1790 could have imagined: they could be a railroad engineer, a telegrapher, a sewing machine operator, a photographer, a fireman or policeman, a riverboat pilot . . .

Most of her grandchildren and great-grandchildren went to school: free public grade-school education was now the law in most states. College was still ex-pensive, but by 1850 it had become available to many more people—including, in a limited form, women.

Most women still married and kept house, as they had when she was growing up. But that was no longer their only choice. Like men, they could earn their own living in factories, shops, or offices, or in new fields that women dominated, like education and nursing. True, their pay was lower and their choices were fewer than those of men, but compared with life in 1790, women had more opportunities for a variety of jobs.

The United States in 1850 was no earthly paradise. Small children still worked long hours in factories and mines. Though industry made the United States wealthy, the wealth was not evenly spread around. Workers who tried to unite to press for better pay and treatment had an uphill battle. New immigrants from Europe were crowded in the unhealthful city slums, cut off from American life by their languages and customs. Often, their bosses took advantage of them, paying them less and working them harder than native-born Americans.

As the United States became an industrial nation, other people suffered too. Native Americans were seen as obstacles in the way of the country's expansion. They were driven from their homes and forced onto reservations, on land nobody else wanted.

Cotton was the raw material for much of the nation's industrial growth. It could be drawn and spun and woven on high-speed machines, but it had to be planted and tended and picked in the old, slow way. That work was done by slaves on the plantations of the South. Much of the new industry bypassed the South. It had few factories, few railroads; it remained more agricultural

The interior of a nineteenth-century steel mill.

Bales of cotton await shipment from New Orleans to the mills of the North.

As the Civil War begins, a Maine mill calls for girls and boys to work making tent cloth.

than the North. Cotton was its main product. As the mills of New England needed more and more cotton, southern planters depended more and more on slave labor. As new lands opened up in the West, southerners wanted slavery to be legal there.

Meanwhile, in the North, feeling against slavery grew. Many northerners did not notice—or did not care to notice—that their economy, too, depended to an extent on slavery. Northern mills turned cotton into finished textile products, and northern-built ships carried those products overseas. Despite this dependency, the split between the busy, industrial North and the slave-based, agricultural South grew wider and wider until the Civil War broke out in 1861.

The growth of American industry brought problems, but more than that, it brought opportunities. It gave Americans more choices—of how and where to live, how to make and spend their money. The woman of 1850 might remember the day when, as a girl, she started tending her spinning machine. Looking around her, she might be amazed by the changes that had come in the sixty years since that day. We have to wonder if she knew that she, just as much as a wilderness scout or a family heading west in a covered wagon, was a pioneer; that she and Samuel Slater had changed the world.

INDEX

Page numbers in *italics* indicate illustrations.

SUGGESTED READING

CUNLIFFE, MARCUS. *The Nation Takes Shape, 1789-1837*. Chicago: University of Chicago Press, 1960.

GRONER, ALEX. *The American Heritage History of American Business*. New York: American Heritage Publishing Company, 1972.

LAURIE, BRUCE. *Artisans Into Workers: Labor in Nineteenth-Century America*. New York: Hill & Wang, 1989.

McDONALD, FORREST. *Hamilton*. New York: W. W. Norton & Co., 1982.

MOSCOW, HENRY. *Thomas Jefferson and His World*. Mahwah, New Jersey: Troll Associates, 1989.

RAYBACK, JOSEPH G. *A History of American Labor*. New York: Macmillan, 1966.